A Haunting at Hartwell Hall

Rachel Bowdler

Copyright © 2021 Rachel Bowdler

All rights reserved

The characters and events portrayed in this book are fictitious. Any similarity to real persons, living or dead, is coincidental and not intended by the author.

No part of this book may be reproduced, or stored in a retrieval system, or transmitted in any form or by any means, electronic, mechanical, photocopying, recording, or otherwise, without express written permission of the publisher.

ISBN-13: 9798480179859

Content Warnings

Mentions of death and the afterlife, including conversations surrounding the deaths of children and the paranormal

References to war and the prejudices relevant to the times in which the book is set

Aggression and harsh words

Minor detail of blood and injury

One

Off to an Awful Start

Blair Nelson's luck seemed to have finally changed when she rolled up to Hartwell Hall on a mild Monday in October. It was one thing to receive an invitation through the post detailing the location — after which she had done a fair bit of jumping around about as it was — but another completely to see the grand estate in the flesh.

And grand, it was. Surrounded by acres upon acres of pretty garden patches and gold-tinged trees, evenly mowed fields littered with fallen leaves, and a fountain spurting out clear water, Hartwell Hall loomed like a proud soldier receiving his medals in the midday sun. Blair couldn't remember ever seeing such an enormous or wondrous establishment before. The properties that she was usually called to were rundown mills stained by memories of terrible machinery accidents or, at best, the tired, cramped, damp-riddled rooms overseeing the murky canals of Birmingham, where lingering, lonely spirits of addicts and widowers lived.

But Hartwell was neither rundown nor tired, and she doubted very much that she would find damp on the walls, either. Blair didn't often pay interest to architecture — the permanent gray smog of Birmingham was usually enough to conceal any decent examples she might have appreciated — but with the stained glass windows and arched doorways, the Tudor-style chimney, and elaborately designed points piercing the sky, she couldn't quite keep her chin from dropping with awe.

It was magnificent, like something from a fairy tale.

Blair would not fit in well.

Still, she paid her cab driver with the last few shillings rattling about in her purse, ignoring his grumble when he found no tip, and then stepped out onto the bleached white stone. Her shoes hardly knew what to do on such a smooth surface; they were more accustomed to cobbles and dirty puddles. With a deep breath, she smoothed down her dress, though it did little to get rid of the wrinkles caused by the four-hour journey here — and stilled.

The house seemed to breathe with her — *sigh* with her, as though welcoming her home. Blair had been summoned to dozens of different places, but never had she felt something before even stepping inside.

To confirm it wasn't just wishful thinking, she pressed her fingers onto the red brick and held her breath. It was cool and rough against her skin, and... she was certain that she felt a faint pulse somewhere in the stone. Something lived in these walls.

A shudder scuttled down Blair's spine.

She was reluctant to pull away, but her driver had pulled her battered trunk of belongings from his motorcar, and he cleared his throat for her attention now.

"Thank you, sir." She gathered the case herself, being as it was light as a feather. Save for the four dresses she owned — or, rather, had borrowed without asking — the trunk was mostly filled with empty space. Not that she could afford much more than that anyway, and she certainly did not have the money for the equipment most people in her line of work liked to haul around to make them seem as though they knew what they were doing. The truth was they rarely did, and Blair *always* did. She didn't need cameras or recording devices to prove it.

The driver bid her farewell and climbed back into his motorcar, circling the shrubs and rose bushes before wending back across the lane towards the wrought-iron gates. When he was nothing more than a black dot amongst the dying trees, Blair sighed and looked back at the hall. It was just the two of them now. No going back.

Anticipation was a restless, living thing in her gut as she dared her first step inside. There was nobody to help her with her luggage, and nobody waited at the front desk, either. Her footsteps echoed against the lacquered wooden floors as she glanced around the foyer. It was... magnificent. Even more so than the outside. A chandelier dangled from the high ceiling, and spiral staircases plunged up onto the first floor on either side of the room. Oil paintings hung on the walls in gilded frames, and three arcing windows that must have been thrice the height of Blair displayed the vibrant gardens at the back of the hall, where a few guests milled and children played on the grass.

Blair couldn't pretend as though such lavish surroundings didn't make her uneasy. She adjusted the hem of her dress again, wishing now that she would have worn her mother's pretty pink silk one with the fake pearls instead of the ratty old thing she'd stolen from Ruth, the woman living in the room opposite Blair's.

Instinct drove her to root through her handbag for a cigarette, the glow of the lighter flickering across her freckled face until the end was lit. Slightly more at ease with something to busy herself with, she decided to take the opportunity to wander around before she sought out the hall's owner.

Whatever she'd felt outside was magnified 1,000 times over in here. The walls hummed, leaving anxiety to swirl in Blair's stomach. Using her...

talents was always difficult, each property and presence bringing something she had never quite encountered before. But here… she had no idea what to expect.

The paintings and frequent drags of her cigarette kept her occupied enough to push it all down for later. The first, hanging by the staircase, was a painting of the hall dated 1833, backed by an unblemished blue sky. Not much about it had changed at all save for the seasons. The building was exactly the same as Blair had seen it, though the red brickwork was slightly less bright now, and more ivy had crawled across the walls.

The second was a jam-packed painting of Chester Racecourse, well-dressed elites of another time, a time of high necklines and low hemlines, soaked in sunlight as they watched the horses and jockeys on the track. And the third…

Oh.

Another chill danced along the knots of Blair's spine, each vertebra at a time, as though she had stepped into an icy puddle on a frosty winter's day. And her cigarette… it had stopped glowing amber, leaving only gray ash and wisps of smoke in its wake. Extinguished.

Somebody was here with her.

Though her heart began to thrash against her ribs, she forced herself to remain calm as she lowered the cigarette and let the cold engulf her. It was her first rule: *Accept whatever comes your way. They've found you for a reason.*

"Hello." Though it was whispered, Blair's low rasp bounced eerily off the walls so that somebody standing on the other side of the foyer might have heard her. "I'm here to help you."

The ice seemed to thaw around her all at once. Gone. Perhaps the presence had been set at ease, now they knew that Blair could feel them and intended no harm. But still, suspicion remained, and she glanced up at the third painting.

It was a family portrait titled *The Hartwells*, dated 1913. Eleven years ago. The top row displayed a sour-faced elderly man and woman and, below them, a slightly younger couple. The younger man shared so many shadowy similarities to the older woman that he must have been her child, though he was brown haired and his features were slightly less intimidating. Below them, two pale teens — a bored-looking girl and smirking boy — with the same sharp, dark features as the rest of their family.

Wondering if perhaps the cold presence she'd felt was one of the people in the painting, Blair disposed of her old cigarette into an ornate plate she hoped was an ashtray and lit another one. She wouldn't like to meddle with such a grave-looking family, but it was too late to change her mind now.

She was only two puffs in when a stern voice sliced through the hall's creaks and groans. "Excuse me, madam. We ask that our guests only smoke in the taproom. This is a very old, cherished house, and the smell lingers awfully."

Blair turned on her heel in surprise, smoke still curling from her cigarette as she sought the speaker. It was a dark-haired, pointy-chinned, hollow-cheeked woman much like the teenage girl in the painting, though older now. Perhaps even older than Blair. Her large brown eyes dragged across Blair's figure with more than a little disdain twinkling in them, and then she pursed her lips and clasped her hands together impatiently.

"Apologies." Blair made to stub out the cigarette in the gold-leafed plate.

"Oh, that's not an ashtray —"

Too late. The damage was done, the two wilted cigarettes lying on the plate. The woman huffed, and Blair winced. "Sorry. I thought it was."

The woman hummed and muttered, "Yes. I can see how you could mistake a 100-year-old antique for an ashtray."

"I can…." Blair picked the plate up to clean it off, but the woman's hands fell over her own, bony and icy to the touch.

"Please don't touch." She pried the plate from Blair's grasp and placed it back down before pulling her away by the elbow. "Are you checking in, madam?"

"No. Well, yes, but I was invited here by Vincent Hartwell?" It was a fact, but beneath the woman's cutting scrutiny, it came out more like a question. "He might have mentioned me. I'm a paranormal investigator, you see, and—"

A choke of surprise fell from the woman, her hands covering her mouth as her eyes widened. Her complexion was so wan that Blair could see the purple circles and veins snaking beneath. "You're a *what*, sorry?"

Here it was. Blair was no stranger to skeptics, and she tried to remain patient as she repeated, "A paranormal investigator."

"Right." Doubt made the woman's tone patronizing, and Blair narrowed her eyes. "Well, I'm not sure what my father might have said to you, but we aren't in need of one of those here. I hope you didn't waste a journey."

It came as no surprise to learn that the woman *was* Vincent's daughter, but it did to find that they were not on the same page in terms of the hall's ghost issue. "So Mr. Hartwell wasn't telling the truth, then, when he told me of the disturbances happening around the hall?"

Miss Hartwell's lips parted, the first sign of hesitance Blair had seen. "The disturbances would be better solved by a plumber than a *paranormal investigator*, I think."

Blair shifted to stamp her foot, growing tired of the snarkiness. Before she could reiterate that Vincent Hartwell himself had invited her here, though, the sound of footsteps pattered across the staircase. At the bottom, a man appeared, identical to the one in the painting in every way but for the silver streaks in his hair.

"Felicity, there's a lady in room ten asking if

— *ah*!" He halted when he lifted his focus from his feet and met Blair's eye. "Apologies. I didn't know you were with a guest."

"She's not a guest," Miss Hartwell replied.

At the same time, Blair said, "I'm the paranormal investigator."

The man — Vincent, Blair could only assume — scratched his head as he eyed first his daughter and then Blair. "Oh, of course! Miss Nelson, is it?"

"It certainly is. You may call me Blair, though." Blair fought the temptation to smirk at Miss Hartwell for proving her wrong. "I received your letter just last week and made my way here as soon as my schedule permitted it."

"Well, how splendid!" Vincent offered out his hand, and Blair shook it politely. "I'm so delighted to meet you in person."

"Likewise, Mr. Hartwell."

"Just Vincent is fine. And this is my daughter, Felicity. She helps me run the hall. Oh—!" His attention was stolen by a maid scuttling across the foyer, clutching folded white sheets. "Nancy, come over here and meet our new guest!" To Blair, he leaned in and whispered, "Nancy is a big believer. She's been beside herself since the trouble started."

Nancy couldn't have been much older than Blair's twenty-six years, though dark circles protruded beneath her pale eyes and her wiry, chestnut hair had been tied back beneath her maid's hat, making her look older. It seemed that not many people got much sleep around here.

"Hello, Miss...?" Nancy began.

"Blair is fine." Blair offered a particularly amicable smile to the maid. She had tried her own hand at the job once or twice when business had dried up and rent had been due, but touching other people's dirty laundry and belongings had triggered too much for Blair. Too much history had been embedded in the sheets. Too many ghosts competing for her attention.

Or maybe it was just Blair who saw too much, felt too much. Even as her gaze locked onto Nancy's, she caught a glimpse of something — a fleeting one, but disarming enough that she had to do a double take.

Pain, lingering across the maid's shoulder like a heavy, black fur shawl.

"Miss Nelson —"

"Blair," Blair corrected Vincent again.

" — is a paranormal investigator here to help us with our... well, our problem."

"We don't have a problem," Miss Hartwell interjected stubbornly.

Nancy's drawn face seemed to brighten. "Oh, that's wonderful, Miss Nelson!"

"Blair, please," Blair begged a final time.

"Felicity, why don't you show Blair to her room?" Vincent suggested. "Room twenty in the west wing should be ready for you. And you needn't worry about your luggage; I'll have the porter bring it up for you."

Blair hadn't thought that Felicity's expression could get much sourer than it already had been, and yet the impossible happened in response to Vincent's suggestion. "Fine. But then you and I are going to have a conversation about this."

And Blair would be quite glad not to be a part of it.

Felicity stalked off without glancing back to see if Blair followed, her black dress rustling all the way to her ankles. Blair's clothes might have been secondhand, but at least she kept with the times. Felicity's plain black skirt and shirt could have been from any era, perfect only for the purpose of attending a funeral being held for someone she didn't particularly like.

One would think that someone with so much money might buy colorful clothes and a better personality, Blair thought to herself as they wandered up two flights of stairs and into the narrow west corridor. With little natural light available, it was illuminated by gas lights tucked into brass sconces. Blair kept her eyes peeled on the loitering shadows in each corner while Felicity unlocked the farthest door on the right and stepped aside in invitation.

Without the presence of her new employer, Blair couldn't help but flash a petty grin at Felicity as she passed her, into a bedroom of disturbed dust and old cherry wood. A desk had been pushed up against the large window facing the yawning gardens at the rear of the house, a bible sitting untouched in the center. It would remain that way as long as Blair was here.

The bed was bigger than any Blair had slept in before — four-postered and covered in more pillows than she'd know what to do with. If Felicity was not still here, she might have jumped straight onto it. As it was, she dragged a finger across the dresser in wonder and then drew back the flimsy silk curtain to peer at the infinite land ahead. Born in a congested city of terraced streets, she had never seen so much open space before. There were not even any factories spewing out their black plumes of smoke nearby. Just… green grass and rolling hills and cloud-spotted skies. Another world altogether.

"The shared bathroom is three doors down," Felicity said. "Breakfast is served in the dining room at eight a.m., lunch at twelve p.m., and dinner at six p.m. After that, the taproom is open until midnight. Eating and smoking aren't permitted in the rooms, and any damage done will incur a fee…"

Blair was barely listening. She was too busy trying to grasp onto something, some sign like the cold spot she'd found downstairs. There was so much history, so much life in every bit of furniture that she couldn't focus on just one. "Are there any rooms or spaces around the house that pose particular… disturbances?"

"Hmm." Felicity inclined her head, deliberating. "This one seems to possess a particularly alarming disturbance at present."

For half a moment, Blair's heart sped up with excitement. Then she whipped around to meet Felicity's scathing gaze and knew the disturbance in question was Blair herself. "Is there a reason why you're so reluctant to believe in the paranormal?"

"Many reasons," Felicity replied calmly. "How much did my father offer to pay you?"

Enough to keep me off the streets for the next three months, Blair almost replied, but defensiveness pooled in her gut and she crossed her arms instead. She wouldn't give the haughty woman any satisfaction, and admitting her problems of limited funds would certainly do that. "He offered an amount that we both agree is fair for my expertise."

A vehement snort. "Expertise? You're nothing more than a con woman. If it were up to me, you'd have been locked out the moment you tried to step foot in this hall."

It was mystifying to Blair that what she felt so strongly, so certainly, was not what everyone else felt. Everybody liked to deny what they couldn't see, to save themselves from having to uproot their entire belief system, but how could Felicity not feel something as strong as the presence that dwelled here? Something that Blair had taken notice of before she'd even stepped through the door?

Brows knitting together, Blair searched for the feeling again now; she found it much fainter but still there, still humming. A permanent fixture in the foundations of the house. Perhaps that was the problem; Felicity had never noticed it because it had always been here. "Put your hand to the wall. Can't you feel it?"

"I won't—"

"Humor me, Miss Hartwell," Blair pleaded. "Or are you afraid of discovering something you don't want to?"

She saw the moment Felicity rose to the challenge, saw the way her shoulders squared and jaw clenched. She passed the bed to stand beside Blair and splayed her fingers against the fleur-de-lis-patterned wallpaper, mouth a taut line. "What am I supposed to feel?"

The world turned to gray cloud as Blair searched deeper, reached out. *There*. There, she found it, somewhere in the hollow between plaster and mortar. Something clawing, something she couldn't understand yet, but something *there*. "Hartwell Hall is alive, and it has trapped something in these walls. Something trying to get out."

Felicity's snort scared it away. "You're barmy. Absolutely barmy."

"And you don't want to feel it," Blair whispered. She didn't know why it mattered all of a sudden, why she could face laughter from middle-aged men and elderly women and playful children and not bat an eye yet have that desperate need now for Felicity to blink away the doubt and just… feel it.

But whatever lived in these walls lived in Felicity, too. She was part of the shadows, part of the pain, part of the hall. A second heartbeat. Another vein under Hartwell's skin. Blair could see that now.

And she would make sure that she found the heart of it. She would help whatever called for her. And Felicity would believe her, sooner or later. She would have to.

Hartwell Hall was haunted, and Blair had work to do.

Two

Family History

Hartwell Hall was most certainly not haunted, and Felicity was furious with her father for throwing away their money — money they had only just managed to save back up again — on a ruddy charlatan with all the manners of a street urchin.

The anger drove her back down to the foyer with echoing footsteps that were sharp enough to slice through the old floorboards, her hands clasped together so tightly, she could feel her skin straining against the bones of her knuckles.

"Father."

Father's silver-streaked head popped up from behind the reception desk as Felicity marched toward him. He knew as well as she did that he was only "Father" when Felicity was cross. She would have to think of a new name to call him when she was *livid*.

"Oh, Felicity, not now, please," he huffed, his

breath fanning a mussed tuft of dark curls from his eyes.

"Yes, *now*," Felicity retorted impatiently. She crossed her arms as she reached the desk, expression schooled into the harsh lines of disapproval her mother had taught her long ago. Perhaps she had preempted this all along and that was why she'd gone off to London as soon as she'd gotten the chance. "You hired a woman who fancies herself a ghost-hunter without telling me, for goodness sake!"

"I didn't tell you because I knew you would react like this." Father flicked through the guest logs, a pathetic attempt at feigning business so he wouldn't have to look at her. *Coward*. How he had survived a war, Felicity didn't know.

"Is it any wonder?"

Finally, Father sighed and closed the book, placing it down firmly on the desk. "Hartwell Hall needs help, Felicity. We won't get any guests if we don't get to the bottom of the disturbances."

Felicity scoffed, bitterness drenching her every movement and every word. "And, naturally, you sought out a *paranormal investigator* before a plumber."

"I checked the plumbing myself months ago. There's nothing wrong with it, and even if there were, it doesn't account for the other things. The faulty heating and the strange smells. The noises and the awful draughts. Mr. Shaw said that he was up until three o'clock last night because he kept hearing whispers and someone running about the corridors!"

"Mr. Shaw is ninety years old and senile," she dismissed. "And apparently, you're not far behind."

Father's lips parted in surprise, his brows knitting together and his eyes glinting with pain, but Felicity was too angry to feel guilt, too. He was a fool. A fool who would cost them everything if he kept throwing their money away like this. If Mother knew what he had become in her absence...

"That's enough, Felicity." Color crept from Father's askew collar up his neck, across his jaw and his cheeks and his temples until he was the same color as Mother's crimson lipstick. Felicity had expected his meek nature to dissipate after the war, after everything he'd seen there, but it seemed to have had the opposite effect. He was still the man who had trouble enforcing his authority, still the man her mother had left for being "too docile," as though he was a puppy and not a person. Felicity had never minded it until now — had thought herself lucky, in fact, when compared to her hot-headed grandfather. "Whether you agree with my choices or not, I'm your father, and you'll show some respect."

But respect was earned, and Father had done nothing to earn Felicity's of late. The hall would have fallen apart long ago without her here to remedy all of his mistakes. All of the debt and the terrible schemes. If not for her, they would be as common as Blair Nelson by now. "She's a con woman, Father. You'd think that, considering your own son is one, you'd know how to spot them by now."

"*Enough*," he repeated, sterner now.

"No, it's not enough." A lump rose in Felicity's throat, but she swallowed it down quickly. No more weakness. No more vulnerability, not even in front of her father. She couldn't afford it now. "After everything Arthur put us through, you would still invite another con artist into our home. Why not just throw all of our money at her now? Why not just give her the *estate*? It would save us the trouble we went through last time, at least."

"Stop it. It's hardly the same thing."

"But it is!" Her hands fell to her sides — despair now. Desperation. It wasn't supposed to be this way. It wasn't supposed to be the daughter guiding the father, the daughter worrying about losing everything the family had worked hard to build while the father watched quietly. "It begins with your naivety, your willingness to believe, and it ends with people taking advantage of that. People we are supposed to *trust*."

A stifling moment of pause passed between them. The hall was too quiet without Felicity's shouts, without her father's stuttering. She could tell she had pushed it too far. Pushed too much blame onto him. Felicity had wanted to believe her brother was better last time too, but she wouldn't make the same mistake again.

Not like Father had.

He shifted on his feet, their identical eyes locking onto one another's. So dark against porcelain skin. So hollow. Felicity didn't like to look at them in the mirror for too long, and it was for the same reason that she glanced away from his now.

"Will you ever stop blaming me for Arthur?" His question came out without so much as a wobble. It must have taken all of the composure he possessed to make it so.

"No" was Felicity's automatic answer, but she clamped it down to keep from saying it aloud. "This estate is all we have," she muttered instead. "I'll pray for your sake that the woman is as mad as she seems and truly believes her delusions. But if she isn't — if she is here for money — I won't let this house, our *home*, slip through our fingers again. I'll go against your wishes if I have to, but I won't watch another fraud swindle us for all we're worth. We're smarter than that."

Father bowed his head, lids shuttering. "She isn't Arthur, Felicity."

"They're *all* Arthur." And his first mistake was not seeing it.

Felicity hated to be so cynical. She hated that she searched every person she met for some sign of ulterior motives, hated that she saw everyone in terms of what they might take from her. But there was too much at stake, too much to protect, and if her own brother could lie and steal from her, what was to stop anyone else doing the same?

It was Arthur who had made her this way.

After the war, he'd been distant, always traveling, until he'd returned once last summer. Felicity had ignored the signs — the bleary eyes and the constant stench of liquor lacing his breath — and given him money when he'd asked. For a new business venture, he'd said, or to hire a mechanic to fix his motorcar or to invest in a new property. He had made himself helpful around Hartwell too, always seeing to guests and running the business side of things. But every night, he would disappear until dawn, and Felicity didn't know why. And then things started to go missing: guests' valuables, their mother's old ornaments, Father's war medals, Grandfather's pocket watch. It took a while to understand why, until one of the porters claimed to have seen Arthur in town, drinking and gambling away hundreds of pounds.

When Felicity confronted him, he'd promised to stop. He said he would pay back what he owed. Father was the one to let him stay, let him keep on as though nothing was wrong. But everything was wrong, and Arthur proved it when Father gave him the savings to put into the bank. Arthur never came back, and the accountant called the next day telling them that every penny was gone.

It wasn't really the money that Felicity hated to lose. It was the trust, the not knowing who might turn up next pretending to be a friend or a guest just to humiliate them, to take advantage of them. So she stopped giving people the opportunity to do so. Father, though... he still trusted too easily. He invested his money in places he shouldn't, trusted his staff with valuables and savings just as he had with Arthur. And now this. A bloody paranormal investigator. A charlatan. They'd only just found their stability and security again, and he was quite ready to throw it away at the first person he found posing as something he thought he needed.

"Mr. Hartwell!" The voice pierced through Felicity's train of thought. She dried off her clammy palms and smoothed down her features before turning with a polite smile. A guest witnessing a family dispute wouldn't be good for business.

The guest in question was Mrs. Walters, the elegant wife of a local politician and a very important guest who would give them this month's profit alone just from the tab she kept in the taproom.

"Good afternoon, Mrs. Walters." Father was as talented as Felicity at pasting on a polite smile. He straightened from the desk with ease, his charm a tangible thing that often reminded her of Arthur. "Is all well today?"

All did not appear well to Felicity. Mrs. Walters sported an expression that was positively wrathful, her pink lipstick-stained mouth tugging down at the corners and her high cheekbones flushed with fury. She brushed straight past Felicity with little acknowledgement, pinching the corner of her wrinkling gloves to straighten them out. "Do you employ thieves, Mr. Hartwell?"

"I'm sorry?"

"Are you?"

Uncertainly, Father glanced toward Felicity and cleared his throat. Felicity took it as her cue to step in. "I'm sorry, Mrs. Walters. Is there some sort of problem?"

"Well, you tell me." Mrs. Walters gave a lofty sniff, her blonde curls bouncing as she turned to Felicity. "My son's antique music box has been taken from my room. He can't sleep without listening to it, and it was inherited from his late grandmother — the only memory he has left of her, the poor thing!"

"I'm terribly sorry to hear that." Felicity feigned sympathy, though she had bigger things to worry about than the forsaken music box that Frank Walters had been winding up over and over again since their arrival last Tuesday. Frankly, Felicity hoped it was never found. "We'll have someone look for it right away. I can assure you that none of our staff would have taken it. We make sure only to employ the most trustworthy individuals, and—"

Mrs. Walters lifted a hand to cut Felicity off. The diamond bracelet clasped around her wrist glinted against the light, enough to nearly blind Felicity. "That isn't all. There's a strange smell in our room, too, and it's making my husband feel terribly ill. And if being poisoned by whatever fumes you're setting free in this place isn't enough, the lovely flowers that my husband bought me yesterday have already wilted!"

Felicity frowned. She wasn't sure how she was to blame for dead flowers, and she was certain that any funny smells had probably emanated from Mr. Walters himself, given the three-course meals with extra cabbage and broccoli he ordered every evening. "Well, I will be sure to have one of the maids take a look at the room soon, and I'll make sure everyone keeps an eye out for the music box. I'm sorry you've had such a... *traumatic* day, and I do hope it improves." The words were laced with a satire Felicity hoped Mrs. Walters would not recognize.

Of course, she didn't, too busy tutting and plumping up her ringlets to mind. "You can imagine that my husband and I are *very* disappointed. This guesthouse was recommended to us by Councillor Lees personally, and..."

Felicity stopped listening after that, instead searching the foyer for a maid to see to Mrs. Walters' room. Fastidious guests with too much time on their hands were exactly the reason why Father had hired the red-haired woman upstairs, so she would let *him* deal with the fallout of this one. Maybe Miss Nelson would be quite glad to hear of the stolen music box and strange odor.

Either way, Felicity wanted no part in it, so she wandered out of the foyer to find Nancy and prepare the dining room for an evening meal instead.

Three

The Maid's Request

The dining room might as well have been a ballroom for all of its size and plush decor. There was an empty stage at the far side of the room, and Blair hoped she might get to experience some live jazz while she was here. For now, the only music came from the soft, dulcet tones drifting through the gramophone, which was mostly overpowered by the scraping of knives and forks and conversation that, after a few rounds of wine and whiskey, soon became raucous peals of laughter from the groups of guests.

Blair had positioned herself in the corner by the window. She liked to be on the edge of it all, liked to be able to overlook the goings-on without being dragged into it. A natural-born observer — but then, it came with the territory.

Felicity Hartwell was doing a very good job of ignoring her. Whenever she appeared from the foyer or the kitchen or hunched over the gramophone to change the record because it kept letting out an awful crackle, her cool brown eyes slid straight over Blair, pointy chin jutting into the air. Blair had never seen brown eyes that could be cool before; they were usually so warm, like the colors of autumn outside.

But these were not of autumn. These were of winter, stripped from the bark of skeletal, leafless, frost-bitten trees, and they were desperate to cut straight through Blair.

"Good evening, Blair. There's somebody I'd like to introduce you to." The voice stole her attention away from the youngest Hartwell — and placed it on the two oldest. It was Vincent who had spoken, but beside him… there could be no mistaking the beak nose and pure white hair of the man hovering at the edge of her dining table as belonging to anyone but the senior Hartwell in the family portrait hanging on the wall in the foyer. He had been disarming to look at in oils, but in person, a jolting, icy spark rushed through Blair, and she almost choked on the slightly dry mouthful of chicken she had been chewing.

She swallowed the food down quickly and dabbed at her mouth with her handkerchief, smearing her deep red lipstick off with the grease. It felt odd to be sitting in the two men's shadows, so she stood, the chair legs squealing against the glossy floorboards as she did.

"Sorry," she apologized with a wince. "I was in a world of my own. You must be…"

"My father," Vincent finished for her. "Harold Hartwell."

"Yes, of course." Blair smiled, revealing the shilling-size gap between her two front teeth, and held her hand out amicably. "A pleasure, Mr. Hartwell."

Harold's eyes skimmed over Blair's extended hand in vague disapproval and then fell back to Vincent. "And is there a reason why you dragged me from my dinner to introduce me to this... well, I dare not judge what she is."

"Miss Nelson is an... investigator... here to... investigate," Vincent stuttered out awkwardly.

Blair almost rolled her eyes. She had never heard such fine mincing of words. "Indeed, your son informs me of the recent disturbances reported by guests, and I came to offer my expertise."

Harold raised a bushy, cruelly arched brow, tongue slipping over wrinkled lips. "They're surely not allowing women to work for Scotland Yard now."

"Oh, no, God forbid." Sarcasm fringed Blair's tone. She had a feeling that she would not get along well with a man afraid of women in power. "My line of work is in the paranormal."

The world froze for a moment, and Harold with it. The din of conversation lowered, the gramophone's music faded, the light outside seemed to dim — and then Harold's face turned a bright shade of beetroot red, jowls and all. "What on *earth* have you brought this woman here for, boy?"

Vincent flinched against the sharp words and scratched at his five o'clock shadow nervously. "Well, what else was I supposed to do? Everybody is certain the place is..." He glanced around and lowered his voice. "... *haunted*, and Nancy recommended—"

"*Nancy*? The bloody maid?" Harold repeated incredulously. "There's a reason her job is to walk around with a feather duster while *you* manage the estate."

At the raised voices, the diners had ceased their chatter to gawp at the spectacle, and Blair could do nothing but rock on her heels and wait for the second Hartwell argument of the day to be over. There was more drama to be witnessed here than with her landlord and tenants in bloody Birmingham.

It was also becoming quite apparent that wealthy people did not like to admit they had paranormal problems.

"*Granddad.*" It was Felicity who dared scold Harold now, having halted folding her napkins a few tables over to pinch her grandfather's arm. "Not in front of the guests, please."

"This is my property, and I'll shout if I bloody well feel like it!" Harold continued. "Did you know about this?"

"No. Not until today." Blair didn't miss the biting glare thrown her way. "Believe me, I'm not happy about it, either."

"Look, I'm not here to cause any trouble," Blair interjected, lifting her hands in surrender. Harold looked at them as though they were holding a decaying carcass. "You won't even notice me. I'm just here to see if I can find a reason for all of the strange goings-on reported recently, and if I can, it means I can help. It's really quite common to find that, in a building as old as this one, a few spirits have gotten trapped on their way across the veil, and—"

"Oh, what a load of poppycock." Spittle flew from Harold's tongue. "The only spirit needing to leave this house is *you*. Now get your things and go."

"*Granddad!*" Even Felicity sounded appalled by the elder man's venom, which was at least a little bit reassuring. Blair couldn't pretend that, with Harold towering over her and the entire dining room staring, she didn't feel slightly intimidated, though she kept her jaw set and shoulders square in an attempt not to show it.

"No. She's not welcome here."

"Well, she's staying." It was Vincent who said it, defiant and without fear. Though he hadn't shouted, everybody's attention flickered to him. And he matched their stares with a blazing one of his own, a powerful muscle quivering in his jaw. Far removed from the kind man who had greeted Blair this morning. "I run Hartwell now. That means I make decisions, and I decide that Miss Nelson—"

"Blair," Blair corrected quietly.

"—*Blair* stays. Now, this is not how we treat our guests, so we'll have no more bickering about the matter. I didn't come home from bloody France just to put up with all this bickering."

Vincent left it at that, whipping around on his heel and marching out of the dining room like the soldier he had once been. And as pacifistic as Blair was, she admired him for it.

She tucked an escaping strand of copper hair from her eyes as she looked back at a stunned Felicity and Harold with newfound confidence — and was met with ice. Not just because of Harold and his attitude toward her, but something else too, something that hollowed her out, left her shivering. Looking at Harold... it was like watching a solar eclipse. Something leached the light and the warmth from the room. Something that hung around Harold's neck.

Whatever it was Blair felt here, it came from him. From Harold. She saw that now, without the distractions and the shouting and the need to defend herself. It was enough to make her gasp, but not enough to tell him. Not yet.

"I... I think I'll retire to my room. Thank you for dinner." She left without another word, but even with distance put between her and Harold, she still felt it. It followed her as it followed him. It followed everyone in this house. Blair couldn't get a grasp on who or what or why it was yet, but she would.

The gaslights guttered slightly as she made her way down the corridors, still breathless from the stairs. If she carried on this way, exerting herself after unfinished meals, she would have to buy new, smaller dresses with the money Vincent gave her. *Better rectify it with biscuits to prevent such a thing.*

On her way to her room, she caught a glimpse of a white skirt poking out of an open door — a linen closet, Blair realized as she drew closer and found the skirts to belong to the maid she had met earlier. She couldn't get past with the door open and the caddy of cleaning products in the way, so she cleared her throat politely and waited for Nancy to notice her.

She did, looking flustered and out of sorts as she turned. "Oh. I do apologize, Miss—"

"Blair, please, Nancy," Blair huffed. Miss Nelson was her mother. Blair didn't want to be Miss Nelson, and she certainly didn't feel entitled to such formal modes of address.

"Sorry." Nancy chewed on her bottom lip. "Blair, it is."

She hustled quickly to roll the caddy out of the way, and Blair made to pass — but something stopped her. The memory of Vincent introducing the maid earlier. "Mr. Hartwell said that you're a believer. Is that true, Nancy?"

"Well." Nancy wrung out a cleaning rag with a self-conscious chuckle. "Yes. Yes, I am."

At least Blair could have a decent conversation with *someone* in Hartwell. "And have you ever encountered anything... abnormal here?"

Hesitation flitted briefly across Nancy's drawn features. "Miss Hartwell said it was probably my mind playing tricks on me...."

"Miss Hartwell lacks imagination," Blair replied. And then, softer, "Please tell me. It's why I'm here. You'd be surprised at the stories I've heard."

"Well... sometimes I hear things." Nancy let out a breath as though it relieved her to be able to admit it. "Mostly at night, but not always. In the east wing, it is, on the first floor. A sort of laugh, high-pitched like a child's. And sometimes I could swear there's a little boy running around the corridors, but when I look, he's gone. Only ever see him out of the corner of my eye."

Blair's forehead lined with interest, and she stepped closer without intending to. "Did you ever experience things like that before you started working here?"

Nancy shrugged, but that intense, crumpled frown remained set on her face. "Maybe when I was younger. I don't know."

"You *do* know," Blair corrected sympathetically. Other than with her mother, she had spent her life being told that what she felt, saw, heard wasn't real. That what she *knew* wasn't real. She could feel that same loneliness swathing Nancy like a blanket and wanted nothing more than to pull it off. "I know, too. I've felt things like that my whole life. It's real, Nancy, and you're under no obligation to water it down because some people don't want to see it."

Nancy's ice blue eyes glittered, her chin wobbling as though about to cry. "Is that how you became an investigator?"

"Yes. It wasn't something I could ever ignore."

"Are you..." She swallowed a breath as though debating whether she should say it or not. Finally, she did. "Are you a medium, too? Do you... feel things?"

"I suppose I am, yes. It's never that simple, though. I can't always find what people want me to find. It's easier to do it this way — search properties instead of people. I find that places often hold more footprints and patience."

"I understand..." Nancy bit her lip timidly. "Would you be willing to do a reading for me?"

The question fell from her in a burst, and Blair blinked through her surprise in an effort to process it. "What sort of reading?"

Nancy's attention darted reluctantly around as though checking for witnesses, and then she pinched Blair's elbow between her fingers and dragged her into the closet. The acrid smell of bleach and mustiness was trapped inside with them as the maid shut the door, leaving them in a darkness broken only by a small slat of light pouring in through an envelope-size window.

Blair was so taken aback that she could say nothing, *do* nothing, only furrow her brows as

Nancy took another heaving breath. They were so close that Blair felt her chest brush against Nancy's, felt their hot breaths mingle, and to be so close to another soul might have left her tingling was she not being held hostage among the linens.

"The thing is…" Nancy began again finally. "I lost a child."

Oh, no. Dread filled Blair, and then pain and then guilt for being so selfish as to think of her own feelings before Nancy's. But had she not already seen the shadows clinging onto Nancy earlier? Had some part of her not already known there was loss sewn onto her shoulders? Blair should have expected this. If she was a medium like Nancy wished her to be, she would have, but using her gifts on people without consent had always felt like an invasion of privacy, and as a child, she'd learned things about people she would have been better off not knowing. Better to ignore these things until they were needed.

"Nancy…." Blair whispered, but that was all she could say. All she could think to say. She was somebody who dealt with grief every day and still had nothing to give but a pathetic enunciation of the maid's name.

"He was only three, but he was ill. For all of his life, he was ill." Nancy's voice broke, and she bowed her head, tears dripping like jewels from her cheeks. "I know that nothing will make it better, and I know I can't expect you to do this for me, but I only ever wanted one more moment with him — just to know he's okay. Could you try? Please, Blair. Is that something you could do?"

Her hands gripped Blair's desperately, but Blair couldn't grip back, not at first. Panic was a malevolent phantom in her gut, rattling around and disturbing the peace. She didn't like to do readings. She didn't like to commune with those who had not drawn her attention first. She should have said no.

But Nancy was looking at her, doe-eyed and shattered, a mother without a child, and Blair was the only one who could give her peace, closure.

So she nodded. She nodded like the fool she was, and she squeezed Nancy's hands reassuringly. "Yes. I can try. When?"

"I finish my duties at ten o'clock. The staff quarters are downstairs, on the east wing. You can find me in room four."

Blair released a ragged breath, steeling herself for tonight. It wouldn't be easy, but there was no getting out of it now.

"Okay," she agreed. "I'll find you."

Heaven only knew what else she would find.

Four

Mrs. Walters' Minor Fright

Nancy's room might as well have been a prison cell for all the likeness it shared with the guest rooms. The walls were pale and off-white, mottled where the paper peeled to reveal patches of plaster. The only pieces of furniture she had were a single bed, a dresser missing two drawers, and a small mirror. It made Blair's blood boil. How could she manage with so little in a house that had so much?

Nancy hovered like a lost traveler in the center of it all, scratching her palms nervously. "Thank you for coming."

Blair closed the door to shut out the draught slipping in from the hallway and nodded. She hadn't felt as though she had a choice. She never did when people asked for her help. It was the least she could offer, even if a reading usually left her exhausted for days. That, and it felt as though a new scar was added to her growing collection each time. There was always a new tragedy to face, a new trauma to heal from, though they weren't really hers to claim.

They felt like hers, though. They hurt as though they were hers sometimes.

"Are you sure you want—"

"Please," Nancy pleaded before Blair could even finish the sentence. "Please. I'd like to know. Anything you can give me." Her eyes already shone with tears.

Blair tried not to notice. "Do you have anything of theirs? A picture, perhaps, or a stuffed animal?"

With a jagged puff of breath, Nancy went to her dresser and pulled a faded, yellow piece of fabric from it. A blanket, Blair realized as Nancy extended it to her. She took it hesitantly, feeling the cold, the loss, almost as soon as her fingers buried themselves in the soft patchwork. It was so small. Too small.

"Please." Nancy stepped aside, gestured to the bed. "Sit. I can make you some tea, or there's a bottle of whiskey I hide under the bed for special occasions. Nicked it from the kitchen. Don't tell the Hartwells. I, er, only have teacups, though."

She was rambling, and it was making Blair anxious, too. It was made worse when Nancy poured the drink into two china cups and Blair noticed her fingers trembling. She fought the urge to ask Nancy a final time if she was sure. Of course, she was sure. If it was Blair, she would want this, too. *When* it was Blair, she had. When her father had been lost to the war, her gift allowed her to say a goodbye she wouldn't have had otherwise.

It wasn't easy, but it was better than the alternative: never hearing from them again.

Things were already spilling through as she sat on the lumpy mattress and clutched the blanket close, and she didn't even have to reach for them. A barrage of images and symbols that had taken years to truly understand, to truly read: the letter E, a stopped clock, a teddy bear missing an eye. And then a cot, a sickbed, so much white before too much dark.

But amidst it all, there was ease. Acceptance. A naive optimism only a child could possess. "He didn't understand. He was too young."

Nancy stopped pouring the whiskey, eyes wide, tired, sunken. "Is he… can you… is he here?"

"He's not here." When Nancy's face fell, Blair grappled for the right words. "He is, in a sense. His presence will always remain close to you. But it's not like his ghost is in the room now. It's more reaching over a veil to communicate with him. I can feel things, see images he wants me to see, receive messages. A bit like sending a letter and then waiting for the response. He's here, communicative, but tethered somewhere else now. Does that make sense?"

"I think so." Nancy's throat bobbed with a gulp. "What do you feel?"

"Peace." A lot of people thought that peace

was a lie Blair told to give false comfort and receive a higher payment, but it wasn't. It was rare that she felt anything but peace in cases like this, when they had passed over the veil. Sickness was something one could come to terms with, move on from, and she could feel that now: the comfort of being rocked slowly to sleep by the person who had brought him life, a lullaby humming through a hollow room. "He was in your arms when he passed."

Nancy's sob wrenched at Blair's heart. She scrambled to pull a handkerchief from the inside of her sleeve as the tears began to spill. It was instinct for Blair to reach out, hold her hand, share the pain. "Yes."

"And it was that that let him know he was safe. That he would be okay. He didn't feel any pain, and he still doesn't. There's nothing more you could have done, Nancy. Nothing more he could have needed from you."

"Then he's okay?" She sniffled into her handkerchief.

Blair squeezed Nancy's hand, her eyes fluttering open again. The corners of her lips curled in amusement as the image of the one-eyed bear came through again. He wanted Blair to mention it. "Yes. He's okay. He's showing me an old toy: a stuffed bear with one of the eyes missing."

Nancy clutched her clenched hand to her chest, and through the tears and the sobs and the pain, she laughed. She *laughed*, and Blair laughed with her. "A bloody stray cat got hold of his teddy bear on the way back from the park and chewed one of the eyes. He cried so much, I had to turn around and chase the thing all the way around Chester, and then I replaced it with a button from an old cardigan."

"You were a good mother. Elliot knows that. He loved you very much, Nancy."

The maid faltered for a moment, something glinting in her eye, replacing her grief. Something dazzling. Not disbelief, but the opposite. "I don't remember telling you his name."

Blair smiled. The name had come subtly, embedded with the other images, something she hadn't even noticed until Nancy had pointed it out. "I don't think you did."

Nancy said nothing, looking at Blair as though the world had tilted... or righted itself, perhaps, just a little bit. That look alone was the reason why Blair had never closed herself off to all of the pain and ghosts snaking their way through her barriers each day. It was awful and heartbreaking to be swathed so firmly in death, as though she had been born in a grave, but it would have been selfish of her not to use it for some good.

Elliot wasn't coming back to Nancy, but at least now Nancy could rest knowing that her son had found peace. He hadn't suffered. In the end, it was all a mother could pray for.

"Thank you, Blair. Thank you so, so much." The corner of Nancy's eyes creased with appreciation, and then she pulled Blair into one of the tightest hugs Blair had ever gotten. She tensed at first, always so wary of what might come through with human contact, but then found that those shadows she had spotted on Nancy earlier today had dissipated, and there was nothing left to discover in the maid save for her kind nature and spring-like warmth.

And then Nancy pulled away and wiped her eyes. "I should pay you. Let me see what I have in my purse...."

She stood before Blair could stop her, scrambling through her dresser and pulling out a coin purse even smaller than Blair's. Blair stopped her with her hand atop Nancy's. "Please. Save your money for yourself, Nancy."

"But—"

"I don't want it. Really. I'm just glad someone in this place believes me."

The harsh creases of Nancy's face unraveled until she looked a decade younger than she had just this afternoon. She still deserved so much more than this: a lost son, a life of cleaning up after people with more money than she could ever imagine having. What Blair had given her was the least she could do.

A shrill scream ripped through the quiet, then — ripped through the newfound peace as though it had never existed at all. Blair's heart stuttered, not with fear but with that damned adrenaline that always led her to trouble or at least the local bar, where there was always someone brawling. She was out the door in an instant, Nancy lagging behind her with her skirt bunched in her hands to keep from tripping.

The lights blinked as they sprinted through the corridor, and Blair quite regretted the five digestive biscuits she'd scoffed for supper — but she had been hungry and hadn't expected to *run* tonight.

Her shoes skidded across the foyer's floorboards as they emerged from the shadows and found the source of all the noise.

A woman wearing opulent furs and pearls, pointing at something in the corner and screeching.

Blair frowned, slowing in her approach in case a presence had come to reveal itself.

But when she sidled up beside the woman, she saw only a button-size spider crawling up the walls.

"Oh, how awful! Get it away! Get it away!" the woman shrieked.

"Mrs. Walters?" The voice came from behind. Nancy turned to find an alarmed Felicity. In her panic, Blair hadn't noticed her approaching. "Whatever is the matter?"

"There's a spider on the wall," Blair deadpanned, stepping away to make room for Felicity. "How traumatizing. How are we expected to sleep tonight after such a terrible fright?"

"*Oh*." Felicity's concern cleared quickly,

shoulders slumping. "Nancy, could you get something to—" She did a double-take upon seeing Nancy's tear-stricken face. "Oh, Nancy, don't tell me that you're afraid of it, too."

"No, ma'am. I'm perfectly fine. I'll get rid of it right away."

Blair pursed her lips in disapproval. Nancy had been working all day. She shouldn't have been made to catch an arachnid just because one of the posh guests clearly possessed a penchant for melodrama.

"Not to worry, Mrs. Walters," Felicity assured, ushering her toward the staircase. It was probably more for her own benefit than Mrs. Walters's. "It's all sorted now."

Mrs. Walters began her climb up the stairwell still muttering beneath her breath. With her gone, Felicity placed her hands on her hips and blew wiry strands of dark hair from her eyes. "Dare I ask why I caught you coming from the direction of the staff's quarters?"

Blair only shrugged nonchalantly, though it was difficult after such a powerful reading. She was still heavy from such grief. "Nancy asked me for a private favor."

Curiosity — or, more likely, suspicion — left Felicity's brow to quirk upward. "She was crying."

"Was she?" Blair tucked a curl behind her ear innocently. The problem was that she was always shaky after lowering the veil, crossing a line, and it showed in the trembling of her hands.

"Miss Nelson, if you are traumatizing my staff—"

Blair didn't bother to correct the formality. She found herself not much caring what Felicity called her, since it was clear it made no difference in the way she looked down her nose at her. "I think the spider caused the most trauma tonight."

Felicity pursed her lips impatiently. "I think the two of us are long overdue a conversation, don't you?"

"I think you said quite enough this afternoon."

"*Please.*"

The plea took Blair aback. She hesitated just long enough for Felicity to make a final offer.

"I just had Mary put on a pot of tea in the kitchen. Would you join me?"

"I don't know," said Blair. "Are you going to kick me out of your establishment in the middle of the night?"

"No." Felicity rolled her eyes. "I would just like to talk. Is that so bad?"

Blair was exhausted and had done enough talking tonight, but still, she found herself nodding. She had no more energy left to argue.

The two wandered to the kitchen in utter silence.

Five

A Conversation by Candlelight

The silence continued until Mary, one of the only kitchen staff still pottering about at this hour, poured their tea and Felicity dismissed her. And then it was just the two of them: Blair and Felicity alone, with only a few candles to stave off the shadows.

This was the only time Felicity ever had to herself, the only quiet she ever found. Guests would still be enjoying the taproom, drinking themselves silly, or else sleeping in the rooms above, and so Felicity always made the most of the rare hours she was not needed somewhere.

Those hours had been disturbed by Mrs. Walters tonight. She could have left this conversation with Blair until tomorrow, but there had been something in the way both Blair and Nancy had looked emerging from the staff's quarters that had rattled Felicity more than Mrs. Walters's ear-splitting screams. Felicity was not the sort of person to ignore what went on in her own home. She would find out. If she had to sit here all night and interrogate the bloody charlatan sitting opposite, so be it.

"Miss Nelson," she began, not before taking a sip of her tea. It was weak. Tasteless. Mary always put too much milk in, even when Felicity requested the opposite. She'd always forced it down her neck as a child too, claiming that Felicity was too petite and needed the extra calcium to help her grow. "I'm not sure what my father told you about Hartwell, what it is you think you might find here…"

"He didn't tell me much at all." Blair stirred her own tea with her spoon absently. Her fingers still trembled, and beneath freckles almost the same color as her rusty, short hair, her complexion had been leached of its usual rosiness. Something had happened tonight. Something more than a spider's intrusion. "Just the truth: that there have been disturbances. Talk of ghosts. Anything else I learn during my stay here will be a result of my own work."

Felicity rolled her eyes at the mention of ghosts. To her, it was an ailment not to be able to distinguish fiction from reality. And that's what the guests' stories were: fiction. Imaginings to make their stay here less dull. Most of the complaints were from housewives whose husbands spent their days tending to business in Chester or else widowers trying to pass the time. "And does your work include interrogating my staff?"

"It was Nancy who approached me, Miss Hartwell." Blair's voice didn't rise or sharpen the way it had earlier, and concern tugged in Felicity's gut at the fact. Perhaps she could admit that Blair had had a rough time of it, what with the way Felicity's grandfather had attacked her earlier. She might not trust Blair, but nobody should be talked to that way. Harold Hartwell was a frightening man in a confrontation, and Felicity remembered cowering from him many a time — as a young girl who had accidentally dropped an antique plate or a teenager who didn't dress as modest as the girls his own age. He was from a different time. A sterner time. And he was the sort of man who liked to belittle to feel more powerful.

Nobody deserved to be the subject of that, especially not in a room of ogling guests as their audience.

But of course, Nancy had been the one to approach Blair. She was one of the first people here to instigate the rumors of ghosts, having claimed to hear noises in the old playroom upstairs before it had been locked up after a roof leak had left the carpet sodden. Felicity shouldn't have been surprised. Still, a line formed between her brows as she pushed the saucer of tea away and clasped her hands together.

"Is that so?" Felicity asked. "I suppose she told you all about her strange imaginings."

"She did," Blair nodded.

But that still didn't explain their peculiar

dispositions this evening.

Felicity sighed, rubbing her palms together to keep warm. The night had turned frosty, and that cold had bled into the house. The icy draught circulating the kitchen left the candles wavering erratically. "What else did the two of you talk about?"

Blair's eyes turned glassy, as though she had drifted somewhere Felicity couldn't reach. And then she took a sharp inhale of breath and gulped down her tea. "Is there a reason why Nancy has so little furniture in her room?"

Felicity narrowed her eyes. "Pardon?"

"It's just very clear that Hartwell brings in plenty of profit. The other rooms are filled with beautiful furniture. But Nancy sleeps on an old, lumpy mattress and owns very little else."

Defensiveness rolled through Felicity, and she sat straighter in her chair as she replied. "Our employees know that they are more than welcome to use their wages to decorate their rooms however they see fit."

"And are their wages substantial enough to make that possible?" Blair cocked her head: a challenge. "Or do you pay them just enough to get by? Just enough to keep working here, waiting on your important, fancy guests, cleaning their sheets and feeding them and delivering their tea while having no such luxuries of their own?"

Felicity blew out an exasperated breath. She knew the staff were struggling. She knew their ramshackle little rooms weren't enough, and she'd be lying if she said she didn't feel a whisper of guilt each time she walked through the desolate staff quarters to her own room. Before they'd lost most of their money — or rather, had it stolen — Father had been insistent on paying the maids a wage well above minimum, but since it had taken so long to recover from the loss, they'd only been able to offer free accommodation and a meager salary since.

With an uncomfortable clearing of her throat and a clenched jaw, Felicity finally responded: "If the staff have an issue with their pay, they may tell me so themselves."

Blair's lips parted, her focus returning to Felicity, sharper now until Felicity felt her piercing gaze biting through the space between them. "I didn't mean to say Nancy complained. It was just my observation. She won't be punished for it, will she?"

The most peculiar thing washed over Felicity in response to Blair's words — something that felt an awful lot like admiration. But that was silly. The woman had a conscience. That wasn't so remarkable. She wanted to protect Felicity's staff after standing up for them. A lot of people would probably have done the same if they were from a working-class background like Blair's. Felicity assumed that was the case, anyway, what with the dull dress and the broad Midlands accent.

"No." It came out as a whisper. Felicity didn't

know why. "No. It isn't like that here."

Relief softened Blair's features, and she sank back in the chair wearily.

Felicity had to ask again. She had to know. "You avoided the question. What else did you and Nancy talk about tonight? She seemed... teary, and you...." She stopped there. She didn't want to admit that she'd noticed these things about Blair. That for all the distaste and disapproval, she found Blair... interesting enough to take notice of.

"You won't like it," Blair warned.

"I'm not overly fond of anything that has happened since your arrival here. What difference will it make?"

Blair's gapped front teeth clamped down on her bottom lip in deliberation for a few moments, and then she shifted in her seat. "Very well. Nancy wished for a reading. I was happy to oblige."

"A reading?" Felicity repeated, puzzled.

"I call myself a paranormal investigator for the sake of sounding professional, but all it really means is that... well, I'm sensitive to things others are not. I can pass through the veil of life and death a little bit easier, sense things, feel the presence of those we've lost. It's not my business to discuss Nancy's personal life, mind. All I will say is that she lost somebody, and I was able to provide her with a certain peace to her grief."

Felicity understood none of it, nor did she believe it. "So you're conning my staff now, too."

"I'm conning no one," Blair snapped, so bitterly that it surprised Felicity. "I didn't accept any money, and I would never profit from someone else's loss. *Never*. Nancy asked for my help, and I gave it to her because I'm the only one who could."

The quiet that followed was stifling, the only reprieve a dripping of water from the tap and the wind picking up speed outside. Felicity didn't know what to say. Blair's vehemence had stolen any words she might have retorted with, and though she didn't want to believe that it was genuine, she couldn't help it. She had spent so long full of distrust, always searching for lies and deceit, always expecting the worst, and yet this woman, who claimed to be something impossible, had snatched all of that wariness away in just a few words.

It wasn't just the words, though, that did it. It was the way in which she said them, so fiercely, as though she had spent every muscle in her body just to make her commitment to her words known. And the glint in her green eyes....

Apprehension fell away from Felicity without permission. Apprehension and a sort of numbness too, as though she had been swathed in cotton wool. Blair, with her distinct features and utter belief in the things she said, had burrowed her way through and brought Felicity to the surface again.

Felicity didn't like it. She felt stripped bare without protection. Rising from her seat, she tipped her now-cold tea into the sink, finding her pale reflection in the window. Outside was nothing but blackness, endless and vast and so much like what had lived in her own heart since Arthur's betrayal.

But at the end of it, a crescent moon. A twinkling star. A flicker of light. Blair's round face, just behind her, waiting to be dismissed.

"You don't believe me," she whispered, "and you don't have to. But it is the truth, Miss Hartwell, and I must do what your father asked me here to do, regardless of what you and your grandfather say. And if I can help anyone else while I'm here, staff or not, I will."

"Then I trust you will do it with as little disturbance to our guests as possible, Miss Nelson." Felicity's throat felt raw as she said it, so many thorns trapped under her tongue. So much uncertainty. Blair had shaken her, and Felicity didn't like it.

"Yes," Blair said. "You won't even notice I'm here."

Somehow, Felicity doubted it. The problem was that she had not *stopped* noticing since this afternoon. Charlatan or not, Blair had crawled under the roots of Hartwell Hall, under the roots of her, and Felicity wasn't sure what might be unearthed.

She only knew that when Blair left, the weight of Felicity's turmoil didn't ease. These days, it never did seem to ease.

Six

The Boy in the Playroom

Blair's investigation began in the east wing the next day: the place where Nancy claimed to have experienced sounds and visions. With her belly full of scrambled eggs and bacon, she took her time wandering around Hartwell on the way there. There was so much of this place to see, and with each turned corner, she seemed to discover a new part of the building. It was an unending maze of low-lit corridors and fancy wallpaper.

There was one room in particular that called to her. It looked like any other from the outside, but it wasn't numbered — and when Blair curled her hand over the doorknob and pushed, it gave easily beneath her hands.

It was freezing. The other cold spots had been Mediterranean compared to this arctic blast. As Blair stepped onto the pale yellow carpet and shut the door, the life seemed to be sucked from her lungs, an ashy taste gathering on her tongue.

The room was large, with a view to the gardens at the rear of the house, but the sunlight didn't seem to reach through the window, as though invisible curtains kept it out. But the furniture, the walls, the room's contents were all incongruous to these suffocating shadows. Dollhouses and toy boxes, easels and paints, stuffed teddies and tambourines… they were all piled on shelves and in cobwebbed corners, untouched. A children's playroom with no children to speak of.

Except for one. A little dark-haired boy, wearing navy blue shorts that would surely lead to him catching his death outside. His interest was in the wax crayons and paper, and he seemed not to care that until now, he had been alone. He didn't even look up to acknowledge Blair, so Blair dared another step and tried to ignore the way her bones stiffened in protest. The carpet beneath her feet was dark with damp.

"Hello," she greeted lightly.

The boy lifted his chin, then, a strange wariness in his hazel eyes for one so young. "Hello."

"Do you mind if I stay in here for a while?" Blair crouched when she reached him, peering at the pages he drew on. The red squiggles were most certainly in the lines, but from what she could see, he was attempting to shade a hand-drawn pedal car. "I like coloring, too."

The boy only nodded, sticking his tongue out in concentration. Blair took it as her sign to keep exploring. She dragged her finger across dusty windowsills and wallpaper bubbling from more damp, the gabled roof of the Victorian-style dollhouse and the figurines propped up between children's books. Nothing but the same yawning nothingness followed her touch, but she knew something waited behind it. A tiger waiting for the right moment to pounce.

"Have you come to help me?" the boy asked, disturbing Blair from finding that sharp-toothed maw.

Blair spun around and cocked her head in confusion. He still clutched the crayons. "You'd like me to color with you?"

His nod sent tendrils of loose brown curls tumbling across his forehead.

Though she didn't much care for children, Blair couldn't resist the hope softening his features, so she sat cross-legged on the carpet beside him — terribly unladylike, but who was here to judge? — and took one of the crayons from the box the boy offered. Violet, to match the collared, spotty dress she wore today.

With a smile, she took a scrap of paper and began to draw — what, she didn't know. She let her crayon take her wherever it wished as she spoke. "Aren't there usually other children to play with in here?"

"They don't like to play with me."

Blair's heart twisted at the innocence in his tone. She knew the feeling of isolation well, having grown up with talents nobody else had understood. And then there was her red hair and her gapped teeth and the fact that she was always slightly plumper than the other children, all things that still hadn't changed. Blair was too fond of sponge cake and biscuits to try with the latter.

"Whyever not?" she asked anyway. This boy had no distinguishable features that she could see other children picking on. He was perfectly ordinary, if not a little pale.

He shrugged. "I don't think they can see me."

Ah. Invisibility. Blair had never been blessed with a talent like *that*, nor had she ever wished to be. Still, she tried to be sympathetic. "Well, it doesn't matter. Playing alone is just as much fun. What about your parents? I bet they'll play with you if you ask."

"Gone."

Blair's brows furrowed at the brusque response. "Gone where?"

Another shrug. "It's just me. And you, now."

She didn't know how to dissect his words; they seemed not to connect in her mind to make sense, and he was still looking at her with those overwhelmingly round hazel eyes like he needed her to agree, to confirm it. So she did. "Just you and me."

"Will you follow me?"

The boy abandoned his red crayon and rose from his knees, his gray socks slipping down from his shins to his ankles as he wandered to the door.

He didn't look back to see if Blair would, just continued on into the corridor.

Bewildered, Blair glanced once more around the room. Something was still off, and she desperately wanted to figure it out… but the poor boy. He was probably waiting for his parents to come back from a late breakfast or perhaps business in the city. Either way, he needed the company.

At least, Blair had thought he had, until she stepped out into the corridor and found… nothing. Where on earth had he disappeared to so quickly?

Something creaked down the corridor. A door on old hinges. It slammed shut in the next instant, and that strange ice that had been strangling Blair since stepping into the playroom thawed. A chill crept down her spine. She tiptoed down the corridor to the door that had just closed and tried the handle.

The door was locked.

She rapped her knuckles against the wood. "Hello? Are you still there?"

Nothing. Only shifting floorboards.

"Hello?" A final knock. But the sounds had stopped, and if the boy was in there, he didn't seem to want Blair to follow him anymore.

She took a deep breath and glanced down. No shadows danced under the crack of the door, though plenty of light tried to spill there. She could no longer hear his footsteps, either. Maybe Blair should have forgotten about it all then, but… the door was cold, and so was the air around her, just as it had been yesterday by the painting.

Something was wrong. Something wanted her in that room. It seemed to sing through her blood, louder the more she tried to pull away from it. She made a note of the room number. Eleven.

"Can I help you?"

The sudden question almost gave Blair a heart attack, and she gasped, stumbling back. A middle-aged man stood a few inches away, just taller than Blair and clutching a leather briefcase. He had the same pompous air everyone else did in Hartwell Hall. "Sorry?"

"This is my room," he said. "Is there a reason you're loitering outside of it?"

His room? "Oh... no. Sorry." She took another step back, but curiosity still gnawed at her gut, still tugged her to that door. As the man unlocked it, she tried to glance over his shoulder. If the boy was still in there, he hid well. "Excuse me, sir. Do you have a son?"

"A son?" The man turned on his heel, features twisting as though Blair had just asked him if he enjoyed curdled milk. "No. I'm here alone. Why?" A glance up and down, and then: "Oh, dear. You're not searching for work, are you? I didn't think an esteemed place like this would permit such... *unsavory* business."

Blair's eyes narrowed to slits. She wasn't quite sure how a simple question had led him to believe that she was a prostitute. Then again, most men she had encountered liked to believe they were desired or had access to such privileges when a woman so much as breathed near him. "You misunderstand. I just thought I saw a boy wander into your room, but it must have been a different one." *Or something else entirely*, she began to suspect. "My apologies, sir. I shan't bother you again."

The man grumbled about how she'd better not and then slammed the door shut on Blair's face.

Blair huffed in annoyance and marched back down the corridor. As much as she wanted to forget about the room and the boy, though, she couldn't. She had never seen such a vivid apparition before — usually, the dead came to her in images and feelings rather than as a corporeal entity — but she was beginning to sense that the child had been something altogether different from anything she'd encountered before.

One thing was certain: Something was waiting for her in that room.

Blair would find out what it was.

Seven

Room Eleven

Stealing a key from the front desk was fairly easy — mostly because Nancy felt as though she owed Blair a favor, and her maid duties allowed her access to every key in the house.

Blair knew it was terrible to get Nancy involved, of course, but desperate times called for desperate measures. Besides, Nancy had been more than willing when Blair told her of the little boy in the playroom.

After that, Blair only had to hide behind a leafy — if not slightly solemn-looking — potted fern on the first floor's landing until the man from room eleven emerged from the east corridor and, Blair hoped, headed down to the taproom for the night. She waited for an extra twenty minutes afterward to make sure he didn't come back, and when the corridors remained quiet, she let herself into the room the boy had disappeared into this morning.

Blair couldn't risk discovery by switching on the lamp on the dresser. Instead, she slipped one of the curtains open and let the moonlight pour in. She could see just fine with everything limned in silver, and she told herself that the shadows curling in the places the light couldn't reach meant no harm.

The first thing she noticed when her eyes adjusted was the three half-empty bottles of whiskey on the dresser. It seemed the guest had been hoarding them from the bar, a fact she couldn't imagine Felicity would be too happy about.

His clothes were strewn from a suitcase on the floor: suits and tailored trousers; shiny, well-polished shoes; crisp white shirts. The bed was made — Nancy's doing, most likely. It was a double, four-poster one much like Blair's, and a few books sat out on the bedside table, nonfiction titles with drab words and business-related concepts that Blair did not have the education or desire to understand.

But there was no sign of a child staying in here with him. Blair hadn't expected there to be.

There was ice, though. Ice and something charged with static. The fair hairs on Blair's arms stood to attention. The feeling was more intense than the playroom, more intense than anything she'd felt so far. The room was lived in, and not just by the guests. History lingered here, and something else, something Blair didn't want to acknowledge yet.

But that was why she was here.

The sound of something scraping paired with a shifting of shadows startled her, and she gasped, putting her hand to her chest. But it was just the bare branches grazing the window as a breeze riffled through them outside, slicing the moonlight into fragments.

The corner of the dresser bit into the flesh of Blair's palm as she steadied herself. The wind's howl became as melancholy as a lone wolf's, leaving the house to shudder in its wake. She took a deep breath, closing her eyes and opening herself up to whatever was trying to get in, whatever lived in this room. She couldn't hide from it anymore.

When the gale outside rose to a piercing crescendo, a terrible clatter came with it. Flinching, Blair opened her eyes. It was the books. They had fallen from the bedside table. She'd been prepared this time, but her heart still leaped into her throat. She waited for more, waited for breath to curl down her neck or fingers to grasp her wrist — the dead weren't always gentle, and she knew she from the prickling of her skin that someone was here with her — but the noise ebbed to a whisper and the branches stopped their dancing.

Blair held her breath. She counted to five and then ten and then twenty, standing as still as her surroundings but not half as steady. Nothing happened. Nothing moved. Still, it felt as though she was being watched. The presence wasn't intimidating, though. It was… welcoming. It seemed to want to lead her by the hand.

So she let it.

She paced over to the fallen books and knelt to pick them up, trying not to acknowledge the trembling in her fingers. One of these days, she would learn, or else she would stop getting frightened whenever she interacted with the paranormal. Today was neither of those days.

Something caught Blair's eye just as she was about to place the books back on the table: a peeling bit of wallpaper behind the bed's headboard, stark white against the cobweb-fringed shadows. Blair should have ignored it, but that was like asking a child not to touch anything in a toy shop. Something tugged her hands to it all the same.

A fine layer of dust was brushed away as she shifted the bedside table away from the wall, leaving her space to examine it closer. Heart thumping, she pinched the curling wallpaper and tore gently, wincing when a large strip came off all at once. "Oh, bugger — "

The curse went stale on her lips when she saw what had been unveiled: a mark drawn onto the plaster. A letter.

T.

It was written in red crayon.

The image of the boy she'd met in the playroom this morning flashed in Blair's mind. He had been using a red crayon, too. It couldn't have been a coincidence. This was him, and he was trying to tell her something: who he was, perhaps. But one initial wasn't enough. She needed more. She peeled another strip of wallpaper, dismayed to find that the *T* remained solitary.

"*T*," she muttered under her breath. "Is that who you are? Tommy? Toby?"

She didn't get a chance to find out. The door flew open behind her, the broad-shouldered silhouette of a man filling the threshold. The guest was back.

Those bloody twenty minutes she'd spent hiding had been a mistake, and now he was back too early and about to find Blair destroying the walls of his room. She thought about crawling under the bed for half a second, but by the time she'd gotten down on her elbows, the guest was staggering his away around the bed.

Blair remained still, hoping that if she didn't move, he wouldn't notice the heap on the floor. She caught a whiff of alcohol even from here and wondered if he was also using it as cologne.

Dim light flooded the room as he switched on the lamp, and her hope flickered away with the shadows. The man was nothing like he'd seemed this afternoon, subtly disapproving and haughtily composed. His features were twisted in anger, now, face flushed red — from the alcohol or his discovery of Blair, she didn't know.

"*You*," he accused.

"Hello again, sir…" Blair searched for a quick excuse, rising to her knees, hands falling into her lap. "I suppose you're wondering what I might be doing on your floor. I, er, was doing a mandatory room check is all. We've had an outbreak of rats, you see."

"The only rat in here is *you*." His upper lip curled in contempt, framed by a dark moustache. "I saw you sniffing around earlier. I wouldn't trust a woman who loiters, especially not one dressed like you. I suppose you thought that if you let yourself into my room, you'd have your way with me. Or maybe you saw my nice suits and thought you'd search for my wallet."

"No, no." Blair clenched her teeth and rose from the floor, dusting down her creased dress. "Sir, there's been a misunderstanding—"

"Who do you think you are?" The man dissolved into a drunken rant, arms flailing and feet stumbling as he neared her. Blair didn't often cower in the face of people who thought they were better than her just because of their wealth and status, but this one was drunk. Unpredictable. Probably used to getting what he wanted. And still coming closer with clenched fists. "Women like you ought to be left out on the street. Dirty little —"

Blair couldn't help it. When he bared his teeth in her face, invading her space and sucking the air from it, she batted him away. The problem was that the bat somehow turned into a slap as it met his cheek, leaving the man to pause in shock with his neck half twisted. A shock of crimson stained his skin, shaped remarkably like Blair's hand.

"I'm so sorry." Her chest heaved with rasping breath as she used the bedside table to steady herself. "Sir—"

It was too late. The man's fingers curled roughly around Blair's bicep and squeezed tightly. She was certain that her shoulder was about to dislocate itself as he yanked, dragging her out of the room and into the hallway. Blair thought that would be the end of it: that he would spare her and leave her in a sorry heap in the corridor. But his grip didn't ease as they continued down the corridor, onto the landing —

"What on *earth* do you think you're doing, Mr. Chilton?"

The voice came from behind. Relief flooded through Blair as the man turned with her. Someone was here to get her out of this.

Someone was Felicity. With her crumpled, dark features and obsidian eyes, she emerged from the corridor as though she was thunder incarnate.

"This little witch was snooping in my room, Miss Hartwell. I recommend you have her thrown out — or better yet, report her to the police."

Felicity had the good sense to look surprised for only a second before returning to anger. "A misunderstanding hardly gives you the right to lay your hands on Miss Nelson. Let go of her."

Embarrassment turned Blair hot. She tried to pry herself away, but the man's grip remained firm, bruising. He could barely walk in a straight line, and yet he couldn't, wouldn't, let her go. "It's fine, really. I… I *did* let myself into his room."

"And she slapped me! If I'd have known you were keeping feral harlots in this place, I—"

"That's *enough*," Felicity demanded. "Mr. Chilton, you are drunk. I fear everyone in the taproom downstairs already knows *exactly* how ill-mannered after a few glasses of whiskey. Mrs. Walters has already made a complaint of threatening behavior against you. I was willing to issue a warning first, but it's becoming a nightly occurrence, and now you've laid your hands on another guest. I have no choice but to ask you to leave first thing in the morning. Now, remove your hand from Miss Nelson. I won't ask again."

Mr. Chilton sneered, a greasy strand of mousy brown hair falling into his eyes as he released Blair and stumbled back. Blair tried to catch her breath, pressing her hands to her throat to feel the pulse racing beneath.

"I'll be talking to your father about this in the morning," Mr. Chilton said. "*I'm* the victim here, and I'm being treated as the perpetrator!"

"*Goodnight*, Mr. Chilton."

Mr. Chilton gave them both a final glare before heading back down the corridor and disappearing into his room. Blair didn't quite know what to do with herself, her eyes darting as she sought something to look at that wasn't Felicity. Heavens, she couldn't look at Felicity after *that*. She'd been a victim of brutish masculinity before

— any woman who frequented her local pub had to expect the occasional incident — and had sworn never to allow it again. But she had been the one to lash out first. It had been instinct, a last resort. He had been so close to her that she'd been able to see the yellow plaque in his teeth, and she'd panicked.

The anxiety hit her all at once, delayed and unwelcome and disorientating.

"Are you all right?" Felicity's voice was too soft. Too concerned.

Blair gulped down the lump in her throat. She wasn't sure what she was yet. "I'm... I'm awfully sorry—"

"Don't apologize for his behavior." The words were icy. Unforgiving. "Men like that don't deserve any more excuses. I *would* like to know what you were doing in his room, though."

"You wouldn't like it at all, actually." Somehow, Blair found it in her to offer a wry smirk. She supposed this was the end of her stay. Felicity would certainly not put up with her after she had caused so much trouble, not when she already had so much distaste for Blair and her profession.

"Well, no." The corners of Felicity's own mouth curled in amusement, too. "But I would like to hear about you slapping him. I've been dying to do it for days myself. I'll have Nancy send you up some tea, shall I? Or something stronger, perhaps...."

After the sour stench of Mr. Chilton's breath, Blair didn't fancy anything alcoholic tonight, and her instinctive shudder proved it. "Tea is fine."

Felicity nodded, about as polite as Blair had ever seen her. "Tea it is."

∞∞∞

Felicity hovered uncertainly by the door as Blair scrambled around her room, collecting strewn dresses from the floor and then sweeping notebooks off the table. She wasn't quite sure why she had offered tea — *again* — nor was she sure why she wasn't angrier about the fact that Blair was now breaking into her guests' rooms.

Nancy must have sensed something amiss, because she was quick to set down the tea and go without meeting Felicity's eye, leaving them in an uncomfortable silence that dragged on for minutes, hours. Blair wouldn't look at Felicity, either, not even when she shifted finally and offered out a chair while taking the one opposite.

She picked up the teapot as Felicity sat, but her fingers still trembled around the ceramic handle, and Felicity swiftly batted them away to replace them with her own. The steam warmed her face as she poured, clearing her throat to ready herself for the uncomfortable conversation to come.

"Did he hurt you?" Felicity gestured to the arm Mr. Chilton had been gripping so tightly. She could only imagine what sort of damage he could have left. Blair was not frail — soft padding covered every inch of her, and she was at least a few inches taller than Felicity — but she had seemed it just for a moment in the corridor. It had infuriated Felicity more than any of Mr. Chilton's other drunken actions had since his arrival. That he would lay his hands on Blair... touch her as though he *owned* her...

Not that Felicity cared for her. It was her gut that had reacted tonight, her gut that had drawn a tight fist, ready to hit out if needed. She despised men who thought they could treat women like toys, and she'd been watching Mr. Chilton do so for days.

The rest of Felicity was still sane enough to know Blair was foolish and irritating and probably a con woman, regardless of the night's events.

So Felicity told herself, anyway.

Blair dismissed Felicity with a wave of her hand and then smoothed down her copper curls, slightly tousled from the incident. A splash of red stained each cheek, though, and Felicity knew she must have been ashamed. "I'm fine. Honestly."

"Alright." Felicity sniffed and sipped her tea before continuing. "Tell me what happened. From the beginning."

"You won't believe me."

"Probably not," she admitted. "Let's see, shall we? I might surprise you."

Blair lifted her brows, unconvinced, but traced her finger across the chipped rim of the teacup and began all the same. "I was in the playroom this morning. I met a young boy there."

Felicity's brows furrowed. "The playroom is locked. How did you get in?"

"It wasn't locked this morning. I just… turned the handle."

"No." Felicity shook her head in bewilderment. "No, it's been locked for months. There was a leak from one of the pipes, and we haven't been able to replace the carpet yet."

Blair's eyes turned glassy. "Then… perhaps it opened for me."

Choking on a scoff, Felicity crossed her legs beneath the table. "Or perhaps you've been stealing keys."

Blair rolled her eyes and pushed out of her chair, the legs chafing against the worn carpet. She drifted over to the window, peeling back the flimsy curtain to reveal a starless night outside. Her features were gray in the watery moonlight. "I told you you wouldn't believe me."

With a frustrated sigh, Felicity dropped a sugar cube into her tea. She didn't usually take anything other than a drop of milk, but she needed something sweet tonight rather than more bitterness. "Okay. Fine. The playroom door magically opened for you. What next?"

"There was a boy inside."

Oh, dear Lord. If the playroom door *was* open and the children had been using it, Felicity could very easily end up with a barrage of complaints about the state of the place. But she was *so* certain that it had been locked. She had double-checked only last week after retrieving measurements for the carpet fitter. "What boy?"

"He couldn't have been more than ten or eleven. He was crayoning in the corner."

"The Walters' boy? He *is* a little fair-haired terror…."

"No." Blair turned from the window and chewed on her lip uncertainly. "No, this boy had brown hair."

Felicity's features twisted with complete bafflement at that. "There are no brown-haired boys of that age staying here. Only the Walters' boy, an infant downstairs, and a five-year-old with the Dawson family."

"Well… I don't think the boy I met *is* staying here. Not as a guest."

"Then who was he?"

"I think perhaps he was a ghost." Blair waited — probably for Felicity to scoff again or else rant about how silly it was to suggest such a thing. But Felicity didn't. Blair's eyes twinkled with such earnestness, such belief in her own claim, that any mockery was lost before Felicity had even the time to find it.

And she had promised to listen. Even if she didn't believe it, she would keep to her word, if only to find out why all of this had ended with Blair being hauled out of Mr. Chilton's room.

"Go on," she urged, watching Blair carefully.

"He felt... lost," Blair continued. "Sad. And then he asked me to follow him out of the playroom, so I did. He disappeared into Mr. Chilton's room, but when I tried to go in too, I found the room locked. I knew the boy wanted me to go in there, to find something, so I took the room key from the front desk when your father was distracted and waited until Mr. Chilton went down to the taproom for the night."

"And?" Without meaning to, Felicity leaned forward in her chair. Blair might have been delusional, but she spun a good story. "What did you find?"

"I found the letter 'T,'" Blair said. "It was drawn on the wall behind the bed, just beneath a peeling bit of wallpaper. And it had been done in red crayon, just like the one I saw the boy holding."

"The letter 'T,'" Felicity repeated, unable to hide how underwhelmed she was by the revelation.

But Blair nodded as though she had just discovered the crown jewels, her green eyes wide and unblinking. "Do you know anybody who might have stayed in Hartwell with that initial?"

Felicity pondered the question for a few moments. They had had hundreds, perhaps even thousands of guests since the opening in 1840. Blair couldn't truly expect Felicity to remember all of the ones with names beginning with "T." "We used to have a tabby cat named Tiberius."

Now Blair was the one to scoff. "You'll never

take me seriously, will you? I'm telling you that I *saw* something today. Something *important*. Why won't you believe me?"

"I'm sorry, Miss Nelson." Felicity pursed her lips, averting her narrowed gaze back to her tea. She no longer had the stomach to drink it. "I'm sure that *you* think you saw this boy, but that doesn't mean he was real. Perhaps… perhaps he was a figment of your imagination."

"He *wasn't*." Blair's arms slapped her sides in exasperation. "And whoever he was, I'm going to find out. I'm going to help him, because that's what I was brought here to do."

Huffing, Felicity slid her saucer away and stood. "Well, at any rate, might you do so without invading my guests' privacy in the future?"

Disappointment washed over Blair's freckled features. Disappointment and something else, something Felicity had recognized in herself plenty of times before. Hurt. Pain. It left something aching in her stomach: a knot of guilt, twisting around her organs. But what was she supposed to do? She couldn't pretend to believe Blair's silly ghost stories. She wasn't a naive child anymore. She had trusted in far more plausible things and ended up being proven a fool.

Things weren't always what they seemed. Not even when one wanted to believe otherwise the way that Blair did now. She reminded herself of that as she saw herself out.

Blair followed, eyes tired and dull where

they were usually full of life. "Felicity."

It was perhaps the first time Blair had used Felicity's first name, and the fact was weighty enough to stop Felicity in her tracks. "Yes?"

"Check the playroom door. See if it's locked."

"I don't see why—" Felicity began to protest, but was soon cut off.

"Just do it."

Too tired to argue, Felicity only nodded. Despite the fact that they were in the corridor, far from any windows or doors, the wind roared with vehement force, leaving the house to creak and groan against its strength.

Blair glanced up as though it was a creature living above them, and then her eyes narrowed. "Is that a door to the attic?"

Felicity followed her focus, finding the square hatch above their heads. It was barely noticeable after years of disuse, nothing more than a raised patch of the same white paper that covered the rest of the ceiling. "Yes. Why?"

A shrug. "Nothing. I just hadn't noticed it before."

A draught seemed to slip from it now, and Felicity stepped away, chasing the goosebumps pebbling her arms with the friction of her hands. "Goodnight, Miss Nelson."

"Goodnight." It was no more than a mumble, and then Blair shut the door, leaving Felicity alone in the corridor.

And though she didn't want to, her feet led

her downstairs, across the landing, back into the east wing, and around a shadowed corner until she stopped at the unmarked door of the playroom. She sucked in a deep breath, hands lingering just over the doorknob for a moment in hesitation.

"Probably just forgot to lock it last time," she whispered to herself, though she didn't really believe it. Felicity was too meticulous for any such mistake.

She tried to turn the knob. Failed. A mechanism clicked back against her force in protest.

It was locked.

But that didn't mean anything. Maybe her father had been in this afternoon. Maybe one of the maids had had time to give it a quick dusting between cleaning the rooms. Maybe Blair had been lying.

But as Felicity walked away, wiping her cold, clammy palms on her dress as though ridding herself of whatever had lived on the doorknob, she didn't find herself content with the explanations. Vincent did not go into the playroom. He had probably forgotten it existed at all. Neither did the maids unless instructed to. And Blair... Blair had looked so convinced of her own truth. She hadn't used a key.

So how on earth had she stumbled into a locked room this morning?

Eight

The Blackout

A storm tore through Hartwell the following night, so vengeful that most of the lights went with it. Neither Felicity nor her father had any inkling as to why. They spent over an hour distributing candles, thankful that most of the guests had been in the taproom at the time so Felicity didn't need to chase them down in the darkness. The guests had just been glad that it in no way affected their ability to consume alcohol.

After a lap around the building, Felicity could do nothing but join them, surprised to find Blair sitting by the bar, nursing a small glass of wine. Mrs. Walters was on the stage, wailing out an acapella rendition of one of Marion Harris's songs. With the slurred lyrics and lack of instrumental, Felicity couldn't be certain which one.

She winced and fought the urge to stick her fingers in her ears as she searched for her father, finding him in the guttering light of Mrs. Hurstead's candle. She was probably chewing his ear off about her breakfast order; the woman only ever talked about food.

Felicity seated herself behind him just as Mrs. Hurstead returned to her husband, glad to take the weight off her feet. "We're going to run out of candles soon."

"Oh, stop worrying, Felicity," he dismissed. "The guests are still having fun. That's all that matters."

"Excuse me." The voice came from above: Blair's. She had drifted away from the bar and now stood in front of them, blocking their view of Mrs. Walters and her dancing. She was doing Felicity a favor. "I was hoping to speak with you, Mr. Hartwell. In fact, I've been searching for you all day."

"I had errands in town to run today." Father gestured to the empty chair left behind by Mrs. Hurstead. "Please, do sit down, Blair. How's the investigation going?"

"Well…" Blair hesitated, glancing at Felicity as though gauging what she might have told him. The answer was nothing. Felicity hadn't mentioned anything of the night before to her father — mainly because she didn't have the energy for another dispute about money and naivety but also because she wasn't quite ready to admit the peculiarity of the locked playroom door. "I've had a few strange experiences over the past few days. I was wondering if you might know of anyone in your family — any young boy who might have lived on the estate — whose name begins with a 'T.' A Tommy or a Toby, perhaps?"

Father frowned, deep in thought. Shadows passed over his ever-creasing features, dancing off the silver streaks in his dark hair. "'T'? No, I don't think so. Not a young boy, anyway."

"Perhaps your father might know...."

As though summoned by Blair's words, Felicity's grandfather wandered into the taproom, his bushy brows cast into a harsh, crinkled line and his white hair disheveled, as though he'd just woken from a fitful sleep. Indeed, he wore plaid pajamas and slippers, looking for all the world like an intruder in the midst of the well-dressed guests.

As Blair rose, Felicity reached to tug her back. Blair's hand was warm and soft where Felicity's had always been cold, and it surprised Felicity until she almost forgot her intention. She gathered her composure quickly, though she still didn't let go of Blair. "Need I remind you of the last time you and my grandfather had a conversation?"

"Oh, that was just a misunderstanding, I'm sure," Blair waved off, pulling her hand away. "I'm good with old people."

Blair's first mistake was calling Grandfather "old," especially when it became obvious that he'd heard every word upon his approach. He might have been elderly, but he had the ears of a hawk — and the anger of a shark plagued by bloodlust. Even cast in darkness, Felicity saw his face redden and lips curl behind Blair.

"*Excuse* me?"

At the gravely words hissed over her shoulder, Blair whirled around and blanched. "Oh... Mr. Hartwell... hello...."

"Didn't I tell you to get gone?" he grumbled.

"Oh, Dad." Father tutted, rising to usher him into a chair. "Blair isn't causing any harm. In fact, she might have solved our, er, problem. Do you happen to know if we ever had a young boy living on this estate whose name begins with the letter 'T'?"

If Grandfather had been red before, he turned as purple as the top of a turnip now. Protruding veins crawled out of his cotton collar and up his neck, the whites of his eyes eerily disembodied in the shadows. "*What* did you say?"

"Mr. Hartwell, I only want to learn more about the history of the estate to aid my investigation—"

"Get out!" Grandfather's roar rent through Mrs. Walters's singing and everyone else's conversation, tearing the noise to shreds and leaving nothing but hollow silence. The guests stared, alarmed, and so did Felicity.

So did Blair.

When she didn't move, Grandfather continued.

"Get out of this house immediately. *Out!*"

"Mr. Hartwell...."

"*Father.*" Felicity's father made himself a

barrier between Blair and Grandfather, placing his hands on Grandfather's shoulders and nudging him back fearfully. "You're being incredibly rude. There's really no need for such a spectacle. It was only a question."

Felicity didn't know what to do. In her twenty-eight years, she had never seen her grandfather so furious. Not when she had broken an antique vase or when Arthur had stolen their money or when Mother left Father to manage Hartwell alone. Her heart thundered louder than the storm outside, and she could only imagine how it must have felt for Blair to be on the receiving end of it — especially after being treated the way she had been by Mr. Chilton last night.

It was instinct to reach out. Comfort her. Felicity might not have agreed with everything Blair said or did, but she hadn't done a thing to deserve being barked at by a man almost triple her age. So she found Blair's hand under the table and threaded their fingers together. An apology for her family's ill behavior. A reassurance that she wasn't the same way inclined.

Blair squeezed back weakly, surprise flickering in her eyes for a moment, gratefulness the next. And then Felicity was left cold when her touch fell away and Blair stood up.

"You know who he is, don't you?" she asked over the bickering of Felicity's family. Her eyes had gone glassy, as though she could no longer see. Or perhaps she could. Perhaps she saw too much. Felicity shook away that thought quickly. "He's tied to you somehow, isn't he?"

"Blair," Felicity warned, steeling herself for another eruption.

"You have some nerve, girl," snarled Grandfather. "You know *nothing* about this family. I want you out of my sight, and if you aren't gone by tomorrow, I'll pack your bags myself."

"That's enough." Father began to usher Grandfather away, his face as pale as Blair's. The room seemed to deflate with relief when they disappeared, though the guests remained silent long after.

"Well..." Blair exhaled a shaky breath, splayed hands wiping her dress down uncomfortably. "That's me told, then."

The anxiety that followed in Felicity surprised even her. Blair couldn't leave. Not this way. She hadn't done *much* wrong, after all. Only broken into a guest's room and prodded a bear who had issued plenty of warnings not to. "You needn't take notice of him. The way he treats you isn't right, Blair, and I can only apologize. You... you mustn't leave on his account."

"Oh, I wasn't going to." Determination sharpened Blair's eyes, making them greener: frosted blades of grass. "There's a little boy who needs my help. Harold won't stop me from trying. I'll pay for a room like any other guest if I have to, but I won't leave."

If Felicity had needed confirmation, she'd

gotten it: in the stubborn tilt to Blair's chin and the stoniness of her words, in the way she blazed all over with a strength Felicity had only ever been able to feign for herself. It wasn't about the money. Whether it was real or not, Blair believed in the ghost.

And for just a second, Felicity found herself believing, too. Not in the ghost but in Blair.

∞∞∞

After two hours of the guests drinking and socializing by candlelight, the taproom's red wine supply had depleted severely and Felicity had to head down into the cellar for a few more bottles. It was usually the job of the maids or Alexander, the bartender, but he had his hands full with the restless guests and Felicity had dismissed most of her other staff an hour ago when they'd begun to show signs of fatigue.

Besides, Felicity needed a break from Mrs. Walters's screeching. She and Blair had been listening to her for the better part of the night, and Felicity's head was beginning to ache.

Her footsteps echoed as she descended the stone steps into the cellar, using the dank wall for support with only a lantern to guide her way. She had hated coming down here as a child. Her father had told her stories of how he'd seen things, heard things, felt things. How he had believed a ghost had made its home beneath Hartwell. As Felicity had gotten older and less easy to frighten, she'd faced her fears head-on and had started coming down before the maids offered to.

But she didn't feel like that brave skeptic tonight. She felt... shivery. The pit of her stomach had furled into a tight fist, heavy and sharp-knuckled and forged from iron. The wind outside whispered to her, the thunder bellowed, and Felicity's heart fluttered ten to the dozen.

But she was fine. It was just a wine cellar. Just the storm. Just Blair getting into her head, perhaps in more ways than one. So she continued on until she reached the bottom of the cellar and searched for the casements of red wine she'd come here for. It was typical that they were in the farthest corner, tucked away behind an old, foisty-smelling couch that Vincent had vowed to fix up a decade ago and hadn't touched since.

The bottles clattered as she slid them from the shelves, slipping two under her arm and holding the other in her free hand.

That should have been the end of it.

It wasn't.

Felicity stiffened as something cold lapped at her neck.

Breath.

Someone was behind her. She whipped around to find out who had followed her down... but only a spider scuttling across the toe of her shoe greeted her. Felicity waited until it crawled off and then stepped on it.

She had been so sure—

A tug at the hem of her dress stole her focus away in the same moment another bout of thunder echoed outside. The combination alarmed Felicity so much that she dropped the wine, all three bottles. The deep red liquid pooled at her feet, seeping through the cracks in the floor. And then the candle in her lantern snuffed itself out all at once, leaving Felicity in complete and utter darkness.

Fear was an oily snake curling around her gut. She could do nothing but watch the smoke curl from the candle's wick, the orange embers ebbing, and try to tame the erratic rhythm of her own breaths against the keening wind outside. The thing pulling on her dress was still there, still trying to pull her forward, but she saw nothing. Nothing but her own skirt rippling slightly.

Movement caught her eye ahead of her. An envelope-size window just above ground level let the deep, indigo night pour into the cellar, the dancing shadows of silhouetted trees slicing across Felicity's face.

And there. A person. A short-framed boy, running across the yard toward the woods.

Who would be out in the middle of a storm?

The pull on her dress turned forceful, drawing her forward to the window. And she knew that there would be no leaving this basement unless it was to follow him. To find out what he was doing in the middle of battering rain and gales.

Lightning flashed through the cellar, causing Felicity to jump back and drop the lantern. The shards of glass joined the shattered green bottles on the floor, but she barely paid them heed. The boy was disappearing further into the forest, and Felicity couldn't let him go.

She heaved up her skirt and staggered back up the steps two at a time, damp heels skidding on lacquered wood as she reached the top and raced through the foyer and then the conservatory to unlock the door and fall out into the night. The drowned grass squelched beneath her feet, threatening to swallow her whole, but she kept on, squinting against the pelting rain to find the boy.

But he wasn't there. The gardens were empty, and so were the woods. There was nothing but her. The rustling of leaves. The swaying trees. Footsteps somewhere close.

"Felicity?"

She whipped around at the sound of her name, finding Blair hugging herself behind her. Her red hair had matted to her face, and her face was dappled with rain droplets.

"What are you doing?"

"I…" What *was* Felicity doing? Had she lost her mind? A storm raged above their heads, and she was chasing a shadow that didn't exist. "I thought I saw something when I was in the basement."

Blair inclined her head, confused. "What was it? What did you see?"

Felicity hesitated, her teeth chattering and her soaked clothes clinging to her. "A guest."

"I don't think so." Blair shook her head and stepped closer. "What did you see, Felicity?"

A lump formed in Felicity's throat. What *had* she seen? A silhouette. What had she felt? A tug. But it hadn't been real. Nothing was here now. "I don't know," she admitted, voice barely more than a whisper.

Still, Blair seemed to have heard her. She nodded, reaching out a hand. "Let's get back inside and dry off, then we can talk about this properly."

As though encouraging them, the thunder crackled again, slightly farther away this time. A moment later, a fork of lightning sliced across the sky, painting the world an electric blue. Felicity didn't know what to do. What to say. She didn't know anything. But Blair's hand was still extended to her, and it was the only thing she had to cling onto in the middle of complete and utter chaos….

So Felicity took it. With a trembling grip, she took it, and she didn't let go as Blair led her back to the conservatory. Because if anyone was going to understand, it would be Blair. Felicity didn't know much, but she was certain about that.

Nine

Time for a Séance

The damp cold had bled into Blair's bones by the time Felicity invited her into her private room. It was nothing like Nancy's, but then, Blair hadn't expected it to be. Though slightly more lived in, with clothes piled on a chair and books collected on a shelf, it was more like one of the guest suites.

Felicity lit a candle on her dresser with trembling, rain-reddened fingers and then another on the mantle of the hearth. Blair was glad it was the only light they had. She wasn't sure she could have handled seeing the fear flickering across Felicity's features otherwise.

"Let me find you something dry to wear," Felicity offered, breaking the eerie silence. Outside, the storm was moving away, the thunder a mere murmur rather than a rumble now. The room still lit up with lightning flashes every so often, giving Blair clearer glimpses of Felicity's pale face.

"Oh, that's not necessary...." Blair couldn't imagine that she would fit into any of Felicity's clothes, but Felicity was already rooting through a tall wardrobe. She pulled out a long, lacy-sleeved nightgown.

"This was my mother's. It should fit."

"Is she...?" Blair didn't dare finish the question, but Felicity seemed to understand all the same.

"No, she's not dead. Just away." She offered the nightgown out and then pulled a robe that had been draped across the back of her chair. "You may change in the bathroom. It's just through that door. There are towels by the sink."

Felicity motioned to a door in the corner, and Blair lifted her brows in surprise. She had her own bathroom. Blair didn't think she had met anybody with an en suite before. She was used to five-minute baths in a rusty old tub and then a swift departure when Mrs. Collins began banging at the door because of her weak bladder.

She was still too rattled to say so, though. Instead, she went into the bathroom and found the fluffy bath towels in a pile on a small stool. Her hair was still sopping, so she wrung it out in the sink and then patted her face dry before slipping out of her shoes and peeling her dress and tights from tingling, chapped skin.

The nightgown was too large for her, an occurrence that happened rarely, and it soothed Blair to know that not everyone in the Hartwell family was so perfectly slim. Still, it brought warmth back to her limbs, the lace chafing her elbows and the silk draping across the swells of her chest and hips. The robe was an even better fit. Blair hadn't noticed that Felicity had a distinct smell before now, but she caught lemony perfume as she slid into the robe and felt her presence immediately.

She found she quite liked it.

Without daring to glance at herself in the mirror, Blair folded her wet clothes and left them on the radiator before emerging back into the bedroom.

She hadn't anticipated that Felicity might be half-naked... and yet there she stood, buttoning up her own nightgown, legs bare and undergarments visible beneath the thin white.

"Oh." Heat rose to Blair's face, and she turned away, squeezing her eyes shut regretfully. It was too late. She had seen the slithers of pale skin around Felicity's ribcage and collarbone, the small, soft hills and valleys between, and she couldn't help but imagine what it might have been like to trace her fingers over every inch and acre. "Sorry."

"It's okay." Shuffling ensued, leaving the candle's flames to whisper with the draughts of Felicity's movements, and then she sniffled and said, "I'm decent now. You can turn around."

Blair sucked in a breath before she did. "Thank you... for the clothes, I mean." Not for the accidental glimpse she'd gotten of Felicity's décolletage.

"How did you find me out there? How did you know?" Felicity asked, perching on the edge of her bed reluctantly.

Blair frowned. She didn't quite have an answer. It had just felt as though she'd been needed somewhere other than the taproom, as though Felicity had called to her and her legs had already been moving to find her. "I just... knew."

"You say you're a paranormal investigator, and yet you seem to act as more of a medium."

She raised an eyebrow and tucked her robe tighter around her body, feeling suddenly too bare, too seen under Felicity's watchful brown eyes. She was shaking from head to toe, and yet those eyes still had not become any less steady, any less scrutinizing, than usual. "Does that mean you believe me?"

"I'll let you know once my questions have been answered."

Of course. Felicity wouldn't just tell Blair what she longed to hear. She'd make her work for it first. "I suppose they overlap."

"Then shouldn't you be traveling with the circus as a fortune teller or offering out palm readings in the city?"

Blair shrugged. "It isn't that simple. My connection deals with presences and pulls, the things that live here and beyond the veil now rather than what may come to pass in the future. I'm not a psychic. I'm just... a messenger, I suppose."

Felicity frowned as though she couldn't

quite get her head around it and then smoothed down the bedsheet beside her. "You can sit down, you know. I don't bite."

"Are you sure about that?" The corner of Blair's mouth dimpled with teasing as she took Felicity up on her offer, her bare feet padding across the floor and then lifting when she collapsed onto the mattress.

She became suddenly aware, then, of how close they were. Of how Felicity's breath seemed to have hitched when Blair had come closer. The lightning might have ceased outside, but Blair still felt it sizzling between them here, setting the hairs at the nape of her neck on end and sending a buzz of static down her spine. It had started as nothing more than a hum of thunder, a sprinkle of rain, this storm between them, and yet tonight, it consumed Blair. She couldn't think of anything but Felicity's fingers inches away from her own, the brush of light silk on the sensitive places of her own body, the fact that she was in Felicity's room, alone, only the candles keeping them from complete darkness.

But that wasn't why she was here, and Blair forced her gaze to slip from Felicity onto the rain-speckled window behind her. "What did you see out there, Felicity?"

Felicity shook her head, pressing her fingers to her temple. "I don't know."

"I think you do. I think you're just afraid to admit it."

"It was difficult to see out there. So much rain and all of the lightning flashes. It was probably just a shadow."

"But it wasn't, was it?" Blair cupped Felicity's hand with her own, desperately reaching for the truth; for some sign that Felicity believed. "Tell me, Felicity. Tell me what you saw."

Felicity's icy fingers flexed into her palms, but she didn't pull away. She didn't break their contact. "I thought I saw a boy," she admitted finally, meekly, "running into the woods."

Adrenaline and perhaps a dash of satisfaction coursed through Blair. "A young boy?"

"I'm not sure. Perhaps, yes. But it was dark. I was probably imagining it."

"Or you were finally seeing the truth."

Blair knew she had said the wrong thing when Felicity's features hardened. She broke their hands apart and stood, fingers curling in the belt of her robe. "No. Enough of that."

"You can keep dismissing me." Blair sighed wearily. "It won't change anything. You and I have both seen a young boy on this estate. He's probably trying to pass on, and I'm certain he's related somehow to your grandfather."

Felicity scoffed but said nothing, just kept standing with her back turned to Blair, elbows folded and head bowed.

Blair thought there was something in that stance. Something Felicity was trying to hide. "Did anything else happen tonight while you were in the basement?"

"No."

A lie. Blair had known when someone was lying her whole life, knew when somebody sounded genuine and when they sounded uncertain. This was the latter. "I can't help if you don't tell me."

"I didn't *ask* for your help." The bite was sharp and left Blair stung.

With a huff, Blair rose from the bed. "Then I'll get my clothes and be off."

She reached the bathroom door before Felicity spoke again. Her voice came out small and foreign and left Blair's heart wrenching in her chest. "I thought… I thought I felt something breathing down my neck. And then my lantern went out and something tugged on my dress. I think I'm going mad."

"You're not going mad," Blair murmured softly, "and you're not imagining things. This is real, Felicity. The boy is real."

Felicity lifted her head and wiped her eyes quickly before facing Blair. "Then what do you plan to do about it?"

Blair couldn't help but let a small smile grace her lips — gladness, because Felicity was finally about to accept Blair's truth. She finally trusted her. Blair could see it twinkling in her eyes.

And she knew what came next. What had to come next, though it was a last resort.

"A séance," Blair said. "I plan to do a séance."

∞∞∞

Felicity thought that a séance might have been Blair's worst idea yet, but she had no better suggestion, so she could only help Blair lay out the candles on the floor. She had no idea what she was getting herself into, only that she couldn't keep ignoring the strange presence in Hartwell Hall much longer. She had almost been startled out of her skin tonight, and if she was honest with herself, it wouldn't have been the first time.

There had always been explanations before now, though.

"Have you done this before?" Worrying at her lip, Felicity tried to avoid the candles catching fire to her nightgown as she sat.

Blair nodded, her face a wavering amber against the flames — almost the same shade as her red, still-damp hair. "A few times. I try to avoid it if I can."

Anxiety spiked in Felicity at that. "Why?"

"Because I don't like to bother the dead. Usually, when they want to talk, they let me know — but it seems this one *wants* to be bothered." Blair's eyes seemed to dance with anticipation as she crossed her legs, her robe — no, *Felicity's* robe — slipping off one shoulder and exposing her freckled collarbone. Felicity tried not to blush, both at the fact that there was something so intimate about Blair wearing her clothes and that Blair's bare skin was butter-smooth and spurred a strange heat in Felicity. She couldn't keep thinking of Blair that way, but it was more impossible not to than ever when they were sat as they were now, knee to knee in the darkness.

Her bedroom already smelled of Blair: a distinct, sweet scent that reminded Felicity of the rose bushes after heavy rainfall. She was all over, would probably linger long after she was gone, and Felicity... Felicity was getting lost in her. It was a mistake. A foolish, absurd mistake. But tonight had been the stuff of nightmares, and Blair was a bronze anchor in a sea of darkness. How could Felicity not expect herself to clutch on with both hands?

"Shouldn't we have a spirit board or... something?"

The question was genuine, but for some reason, Blair smirked. "Do you have one lying around?"

"Well..." Felicity couldn't help but laugh, too. "No, I can't say I do."

"Me, neither. Not usually the spirit board type. This will do just fine, I'm sure."

"So what part do I play in this? What do you... need from me?"

"There's not much to it. I'll ask the questions, you sit and make sure the chandelier doesn't drop on our heads."

Felicity craned her neck to glance at the

small chandelier dangling from the ceiling, still unlit. Another strange occurrence, for a storm had no reason to disrupt the gas pipes. "Is that a possibility?"

"No, Felicity." Blair's hands found Felicity's and squeezed gently, easing Felicity's anxiety. "It was a joke. We'll be fine. Promise."

"Okay." Felicity found herself believing her. She found herself believing everything Blair said tonight. What else could she do? Somehow, she was the only thing that made sense now.

"Close your eyes." The command was whispered, and the hoarse, dulcet tones of Blair's voice seemed to lull Felicity into a trance. She obeyed, lids fluttering shut. "Are you ready?"

Felicity wasn't, but she forced out a "yes" anyway.

Blair remained silent for a few moments, and then her low murmur whispered through the room with the wind. "I'd like to call upon any spirits with us tonight. We know there's somebody there who's been trying to communicate with us. We're here to listen and to help."

They waited for minutes, Felicity's heart a living creature trying to tear through her ribs. When nothing happened, she squinted an eye open and found Blair in the same position, her closed lids smooth with the blue veins just visible in the low light.

"If you're with us, can you show us a sign?" Blair asked finally.

Felicity shut her eyes again. She wasn't sure she wanted to witness a sign herself.

But nothing happened.

"Your name begins with a 'T,'" Blair continued. "You showed me that because you wanted me to know, because you knew I could help you. Let me help you again now."

Felicity didn't know what she'd expected. She felt ridiculous for expecting anything at all. As the minutes wore on, she lost patience with the entire thing. They were talking to an empty room. Blair had fooled her well and good this time.

"This was a ridiculous idea." Felicity snapped her eyes open, anger sparking in her belly.

"No…" Blair's features crumbled, swaying that spark just slightly. "He's here. I can feel it."

Felicity's confusion, her fear, made her snap. "There's nothing here but us: a charlatan and the fool that believed her for a moment."

Blair seemed to wilt as she opened her eyes finally, and Felicity instantly regretted her words, regretted the way they made Blair's chin wobble just for a second before her face flattened to harsh, stoic lines. Felicity had known what Blair had been thinking since the moment they'd met — her emotions were always written all over her face — but she could see nothing now, and somehow, that was worse. Felicity had been shut out, and perhaps deservedly so.

"After everything, you still believe I'm a liar," Blair said.

Felicity shook her head, unable to find the frustration and disbelief of a moment ago. Of course, she didn't think Blair was a liar. She might have before, but... Blair had done everything to ensure that she could stay here, even if it meant paying for her room and facing more run-ins with Felicity's grandfather. There had to be a reason for that. If she was a con artist, she probably would have already made off with their money. "No. No, I didn't mean that."

Wordlessly, Blair stood up, her robe sweeping across the rug as she disappeared into the bathroom. She came out with her sodden clothes piled in her arms.

Panic burrowed into Felicity's flesh at the sight. Blair was leaving. She'd had enough. And after everything Felicity had seen tonight, she'd have to stay here alone, with the shadows and the uncertainty and the guilt for company. She didn't understand any of this. She only knew that Blair couldn't go now. Not now.

"Please." The beg was pathetic, and yet Felicity stopped caring. The room would be too dark without Blair's light. She needed it to guide her, to help her. "I'm sorry, Blair. Please don't go."

"I'm not leaving Hartwell until I find the truth. You needn't worry about that."

Relief washed in and out just as quickly. "So don't leave *now*." *Don't leave* me.

Blair's lips parted with surprise, her forehead wrinkling with confusion. "I don't know what you're asking, Felicity. I don't know what you want."

And for all of Felicity's guardedness and shame and regret for trusting people who hadn't deserved it in the past, she still found herself letting the vulnerability spill over like a tidal wave now. There was something between them, and Felicity would feel so empty, so awful if Blair left her tonight before Felicity could find out what. They were here, in their nightgowns, frightened by the shadows, damp from the rain... raw. And Felicity just *wanted*. "I'm asking you to stay."

Blair blinked. It was the only response Felicity got, so she continued.

"I'm sorry for what I said. Of course, I don't think you're a liar." *You're the most honest person I've ever met.* She inched forward, wanting to reach out and not let go. "I just... I can't wrap my head around all of this so quickly. I didn't want to believe it was true. But I do believe you. You wouldn't *be* here if I didn't believe you. And I'm asking you to stay with me tonight. Help me understand."

Placing her bundled clothes on the dresser, Blair stepped forward too, and then they were so close that Felicity could feel Blair's warmth. It was the only thing Felicity had ever wanted badly enough to ask for it, and all it would take....

She found out what it would take. She slotted her hands into Blair's, their fingers interlacing like pieces of a puzzle.

"Tell me again." Blair whispered it as though

she was awestruck. "Tell me you believe me just once more."

Felicity meant it wholeheartedly when she repeated, "I believe you." And then to show Blair, she directed their laced hands to the left side of Felicity's chest, where her heart pounded so furiously that it made her dizzy. It wasn't just her heart she wanted Blair to feel, though, and a gasp slipped from her when the silk of her gown brushed her sensitive, pebbled nipple. She flattened Blair's hands over the small swell of her breast, as controlled as she could find it in her to be when her stomach was furling into white-hot flames. "I believe you."

The mantra was swallowed by Blair's lips, and then Felicity's hands were clawing through damp curls and she was hop-scotching over the candles on the floor to fall to the bed with Blair. It was suffocating and strange and right, and Felicity couldn't stop — didn't *want* to stop. So she kissed back, and she told Blair that she believed her again and again: in the crook of her neck and the arch of her shoulder, the soft curve of her jaw and the peak of her nose. Not with words. Words weren't needed anymore, not now they had found this new language. A language Felicity hadn't even known she'd been longing for until it had been brought to her.

But here it was, made just for them, and Felicity kept it close while it stayed — all night.

Ten

Followed into the Forest

Somebody was holding Blair's hand. In her half-asleep state, she thought it might be Felicity seeking her out again in the space between them. But as Blair batted her eyelashes open to watery dawn light seeping in through the curtains, she realized that the hand was too cold, too small to be Felicity's.

And her bones... they sunk too heavily into the mattress, her legs slabs of iron and her ribcage weighed down by stones.

She knew what it meant. Something had been trying to wake her up.

It had succeeded.

Blair's neck cracked stiffly as she moved her focus from the ceiling above her to her hand, splayed palm-up on Felicity's satin pillows. Felicity didn't so much as stir beside her, dark hair fanning across her peaceful features and onto the duvet. So long, so easy to knot one's fingers in. Blair most certainly had proven it last night, but all of that warmth and excitement had disappeared now, with something icy gripping onto her. She worked hard to keep her breaths even, though her heart racketed wildly in her chest.

But there was nothing there. Nothing that she could see, anyway. And yet the dust motes had shifted, eddying visibly in the fragmented shafts of sunrise. Blair could still feel the hand in hers. She had a feeling she knew who it belonged to, and the memory of the fresh-faced boy who had just wanted somebody to play with set her at ease slightly. She wished she knew his name, so that she might whisper it, make it known that she wasn't afraid. Instead, she swallowed against the ashy dryness in her mouth and hoisted herself up slowly.

The hand remained in hers, but the floorboards creaked as though the boy had stepped back. And then a tug, an urging to continue forward. Blair swept her legs off the mattress and stood. Her lower limbs were numb, as though someone had sewn her torso onto another person's body in the night. Still, they kept her upright, and she could walk on them, soles pressed against the cold floorboards.

So she did, through the pitch blackness of the staff's quarters and out into the deserted foyer, barefoot across stone tiles, her nightgown whispering between Blair's legs, and Felicity's robe rippling out behind her like a lilac ribbon in the wind.

The smell of her kept her grounded, certain. She was here with Blair, citrusy and comforting and right, even when everything else was wrong.

"What are you trying to show me?" Blair asked finally, voice still hoarse with sleep.

The hand only squeezed. Blair expected him to lead her up the spiral staircase to the playroom or room eleven, but they went straight through the foyer and into the conservatory, where Blair had to adjust her bleary eyes to new light.

And then the hand left hers and the conservatory door clicked, unlocked, and opened to invite in the mild morning breeze.

In hindsight, perhaps Blair should have put on her slippers.

There was no time for that now, though. The hand was back, and it pulled her into the gardens. The rain-drenched grass squelched beneath two different sets of feet, one visible, one not, and the mud clung to the spaces between Blair's toes.

"You couldn't have given me my shoes first?" she jested, curiosity piquing when they passed the fountain and rose bushes. They were heading toward the woods. And isn't that where Felicity had been looking last night when she'd seen the shadow? Blair should have guessed, and yet she'd barely ventured into the gardens at all since her stay began. She'd had no reason to.

Or perhaps she had, and her ghost was only able to tell her so with the strength of last night's séance behind him. Blair had left her questions floating around Hartwell last night, thinking that they had gone unanswered. She'd been wrong. She just hadn't been patient.

A low-lying mist curled around the bases of the trees as marshy grass turned to pine needles and thick black soil, washing the buttery yellows and bloodied reds of autumn into dull browns. A blackbird squeed and gurgled somewhere close, or maybe it was something else. The shrill song was solemn enough, haunting enough, that Blair couldn't be sure.

She shuffled over a fallen log awkwardly, nightgown bunched in her hands. The hem had already turned grubby and frayed, the material not made for dawn adventures — which was no fun at all, really. Blair would have to tell Felicity to invest in more durable nightwear later on.

The memory of what they had shared last night was enough to set her heart stuttering again, but there was no time to daydream about hungry kisses and whispered truths and gentle fingers now. The hand had disappeared, and Blair was clutching nothing but thin, freezing fog. She halted, panicked enough to search for the boy. She listened for the sound of his feet, twigs cracking, but there was nothing but her and a fluttering of wings somewhere above.

And then a smudge of navy blue and a glimpse of a pale face and paler legs a few meters away, disappearing behind a cluster of skeletal silver birches. The claws of dead bramble groped at her dress as though trying to keep her from following, but she paid them no heed, letting them tear the gown instead and using the trees for support as she found the boy's path.

He wasn't there.

A flicker of bright red caught her eye on the forest floor: a music box, unlatched and open. Blair's own pasty face was mirrored back to her behind the lever. She wound it up slowly with trembling hands, wondering if this was why she was here. But if it was, the tinkling lullaby gave her no clue as to why.

She snapped the lid closed to smother the melody and searched. She needed something. *Anything*. The music box wasn't enough, and the boy was no longer guiding her, though Blair could still feel his presence on the breeze.

There.

A heap of moss-infested rocks. A trodden-down patch of weeds and grass. A stone, curved and jagged. Another bout of ice shot through Blair, stealing her breath as though she had splashed her face with cold water. It was a familiar cold, one that reminded her of the first blizzard of winter, when one had forgotten just how awful the season could be and needed the reminder. Only winter was always so full of life, full of light, and neither of those things lived in this part of the woods. Even the birds had stopped singing. Even the wind had stilled. Even the rising sun seemed to have sunk again, leaving Blair in shadow.

Death is what it was. Blair had felt it after the loss of her father. An endless abyss it had taken years to claw her way out of. And the core of it now was that slab of stone buried in the ground. Blair almost didn't want to get closer, but she did, kneeling to clear the stone of the moss and dead vines.

She didn't know why, didn't really understand her own instincts until she found the letter carved there. A solitary "T." Not in wax crayon this time but etched into the weathered stone.

"Blair?"

The voice startled her, and she whirled around, half expecting to see the boy. But it was Felicity who stood behind her, face wrinkled with lines of concern and arms tucked around herself to shield from the cold.

"What on earth are you doing? You're not wearing any shoes."

Shoes were the least of Blair's worries. She returned her focus to the stone, the uneven patch of earth beneath, and she knew. The restless, lost presence of the young boy....

He was buried here, in this airless, lifeless pocket of the woods.

"Blair?" Felicity moved closer, standing behind the stone to examine Blair. "I thought you'd run off because of last night. I thought... what's that you're holding?"

Blair looked at her hands without really seeing them. "A music box."

"Your hands..." Felicity crouched, fingers

hovering over Blair's uncertainly. Blair only realized then that they were shredded and bloody. They should have stung, but she felt nothing. "They're all cut. What are you doing, Blair? What happened?"

"He brought me here. I think... I think this is where he's buried." She didn't think. She knew. But she also knew Felicity was looking at her as though she had gone insane, and saying too much might frighten her away.

Felicity's dark eyes slid to the headstone, fingers tracing over the sunken "T." Her throat bobbed, a devastating understanding passing over her features as she blanched. "Oh. Oh, my goodness. Oh, God. *Blair....*"

Blair couldn't sit here, kneeling on his grave, a moment longer. She pulled herself up on unsteady feet and fell straight into Felicity's arms. Felicity might have been dainty, but she was Blair's only pillar of support in the middle of these woods, and she held strong. Stronger than Blair could ever have expected. Perhaps she hadn't given her enough credit.

"The music box," Felicity whispered. "How did you find it?"

Frowning, Blair drew away, letting Felicity take the toy from her hands to inspect it. "It was just here. I thought this is what he wanted me to find at first, before...." She couldn't finish the sentence. Didn't have to.

"This belongs to Mrs. Walters's son. She's

been accusing half of my staff of stealing it."

"Then he must have decided to give it back."

Felicity considered this, and Blair waited for her usual disbelief, her usual mockery, but it never came. Instead, she looked Blair up and down once more, smoothing down a knotted curl behind Blair's ear. "Come on. I'll have Nancy run you a bath."

Blair nodded, teeth chattering and eyes burning with unfallen tears. A bath was exactly what she needed, and then she could carry on. She *would* carry on. "I'm so close, Felicity. I can feel it."

"I know." Felicity led her away from the grave, leaving Blair to look back at it just once over her shoulder. She made a silent promise to the poor boy she imagined standing there in that sad little patch of grass: a vow that he would be free soon. She would make sure of it.

Whatever unfinished business kept him from passing, Blair would finish it for him. She wouldn't give up until it was true.

∞∞∞

Felicity's bones still hummed with residual panic. Waking up this morning to find Blair gone after the night they'd shared, a night Felicity had never shared with *anyone* before, nor imagined she could… it had been awful. And then she had peered out of the window to find Blair wandering the gardens barefoot, and that disarming sight of her pale nightgown and robe wavering in the dark dawn had frightened Felicity even more.

But it was concern that made her gut churn now, as she waited for Nancy to finish running the bath in Felicity's en suite, because Blair was covered in cuts all over. Mud had gathered beneath her toenails, thorns embedded in the soles of her feet, and Blair seemed not even to feel it. She stared unseeingly at a patch of damp on Felicity's wall, eyes pale and unreachable. And Felicity could only pace until Nancy finally emerged, face red from the steam and hair loose from its usual braid, to tell them it was ready.

"Thank you, Nancy. That'll be all." And then Felicity caught sight of the music box on her dresser and said, "Oh! I wonder if you might also give this back to Mrs. Walters when you next see her. It belongs to her son, Frank."

"Of course, ma'am." Nancy nodded and then glanced at a motionless Blair, worry seizing her features. Felicity could see all the questions that Nancy was unable to ask swimming in her gaze and thought it cruel not to answer them. It was clear that she and Blair had developed a bond of late.

"She's okay, Nancy. You needn't worry."

"I am." Blair blinked and forced a wobbly smile onto her face, pale cheeks swelling in a way that allowed Felicity some relief. She wasn't Blair if she wasn't smiling, regardless of whether it was forced. "I'm fine, really. Thank you, Nancy."

"I trust you won't tell anybody about...." Felicity couldn't finish that sentence. Maybe she had put her foot in it by even mentioning it. Nancy might have thought them just friends helping one another out, and now Felicity had made it clear that there was something more, something forbidden, between them.

It wasn't that Felicity was ashamed of desiring another woman. Not even a peculiar, lower-class one like Blair. In the end, hearts were malleable and they chose for themselves what they wanted. Felicity had always expected that one day, she would feel what she so often witnessed other couples experience in the taproom after midnight. And if that time had come, if her heart had settled on Blair for the time being, Felicity was glad — despite all of the hauntings and the uncovered secrets Blair had brought with her, she was glad. There was so much to discover in her yet, so much beauty and strangeness to appreciate. But Felicity needed time to better understand this all before it got out. She needed Blair to just be hers for a little bit longer, without anyone trying to take her away.

"Of course not, ma'am," Nancy said, brows knitting together. "It's none of my business, nor anyone else's. But... for what it's worth, if I may, ma'am... well, I think it's quite lovely that you've both found companionship."

It occurred to Felicity then that she had never seen Nancy smile before, not until that moment, when her lips spread across tea-stained, overlapping teeth with all of the innocence of a child at Christmas time. It softened Felicity just slightly, and she wasn't able to hold back her own gladness. That she could be accepted so easily by a woman who she knew she had not always treated fairly… it left her hopeful.

Blair's hand found Felicity's. It was ice cold, and Felicity tried to rub the warmth back into it.

"I think it's quite lovely, too," Blair whispered.

Felicity did too, but she wasn't quite ready to say so yet. She was glad when Nancy left them alone again, glad when she could crouch between Blair's legs and take her face in her hands to check her for any more cuts.

"I'm alright, Felicity. Really."

How anybody could be alright after finding an unmarked grave in the middle of the woods, Felicity didn't know, and she couldn't even begin to try to guess who the boy might have been. A guest? A child of one of her members of staff? God forbid, a family member? She wasn't even sure she wanted to know, so to distract herself, she hooked her arm beneath Blair's and urged her up.

"I'll believe it when you stop shivering. Come on."

Blair sighed but let Felicity lead her into the bathroom. The smell of Felicity's lemony soap chased away memories of dank soil and fog-swallowed trees, and she almost longed for a bath of her own. But Blair needed it more, and Felicity made to leave as she began to shrug off her robe.

"You don't have to, you know," Blair said, almost too low to be heard. Almost. "I wouldn't mind if you stayed."

Felicity turned back around, eyes locking onto Blair's as she unbuttoned the nightgown with trembling fingers but not a trembling gaze. The silk pooled around her feet, leaving her bare, and heat swirled through Felicity at the sight of her chest and stomach and thighs, all on show for her. If Blair was self-conscious, she didn't show it, instead turning and stepping into the bath one leg at a time before sinking down into the water.

A breath of relief spilt out of her, eyes fluttering shut, and Felicity could only imagine how much the cuts on her ruined feet must have hurt. After taking a ragged breath herself, she went over to the bath and perched on the step beside Blair's head. She couldn't stop looking at her. Her tumbling curls, the same color as the brightest, reddest leaves outside, all different shades, different stages of autumn. Her freckles. The pink lips Felicity had all but wanted to ravage last night. She was so unusual and so beautiful and so very Blair, and Felicity wasn't a painter, but heavens, she would spend years trying to hone the craft if it meant she could immortalize this moment now, with Blair's head tilted back, the soft column of her neck on show.

They weren't the right thoughts to be having after what they had found this morning. Felicity knew that. But she also knew that for the first time in her life, she was allowing herself to trust, giving her heart away, and this was a novelty she had to pay attention to. *Blair* was a novelty she had to pay attention to. For as long as she could.

"Is it always like this?" she couldn't help but ask finally, when the water had stopped rippling and Felicity had stopped falling. "What you do? Is it always so…"

"Dark?" Blair suggested. "Depressing?"

"Yes."

With a sigh, Blair opened her eyes, lathering up the soap bar and washing her arms and then feet. She winced only slightly, the water coming away murky from all of the soil. "No. Not always. Some spirits are peaceful. They just want to pass on quietly. Others have… unfinished business."

Felicity suspected that Hartwell's "ghost" might fall into the latter category. "How did you find out that you were… more susceptible to these things?"

"It runs in the family. My mother is just like me. I didn't really understand it, not until we walked through a cemetery once on our way home from Sunday mass. I could feel *so much* there. And I saw things. People who weren't really there. My mum told me not to be afraid. They didn't want to hurt me. They only wanted to rest. There was a shop just on the next street down, and she told me to wait outside while she went in for some bread and milk. She came back to find me gone. I'd gone to the cemetery. Talking to an old woman who had died of scarlet fever."

Felicity's breath hitched in her throat. She couldn't imagine such a thing. "But isn't it frightening? Isn't it *sad*?"

"Yes." Blair shrugged, worrying at her lip as she played with the droplets on her hands. "But it's part of life. And in the end, I'm lucky. I get to bring people closure, the reassurance that their loved ones found peace. There's nothing you need more when you lose someone."

"You sound as if you know," Felicity pointed out, shuffling closer. There was a smudge of dirt on Blair's cheek, and she dipped her thumb in the bathwater before using the pad to wipe it away softly. She could have left Blair alone again then, but her hand lingered by her jaw, wanting to just… feel her. However she could. Whatever chance she had.

Blair looked at her for a moment as though in surprise, and then kissed her palm with such softness that Felicity might have been made of thin glass. "I lost my father in the war. I wouldn't have been able to say my goodbyes without my… talent."

Felicity noted that Blair had never called it a gift. She wondered if it had ever been a burden, but she doubted Blair would tell her if it had. Instead of asking, she could only stare in awe at the woman in front of her, the woman who defied the laws of the universe to bring just a few grieving people some peace. Blair could have kept it to herself, kept it all closed away, hidden — Felicity probably would have, cowardly as she was — but instead she was here, determined to free a boy from his prison. Determined to find out his truth.

"What do you think happened to him, Blair?" Felicity asked quietly. "Who do you think he was?"

Speechless for once, Blair parted her lips and shook her head. Color was beginning to seep back into her cheeks, at least. It was minutes before she finally replied. "I know you won't want to hear it, but I do think your grandfather is at the root of this. He carries shadows on his back, and he hates me being here even more than you did."

"I don't know much about him when I come to think of it," Felicity admitted. "He never told us stories growing up like most grandparents do. He always kept to himself. He was strict, too. I never really felt close to him. Maybe… maybe he is hiding something."

"I might be wrong."

Felicity smirked. "I don't think you ever are."

"Well… I'm glad you've finally come to realize that."

Laughter drifted between them, light and unforced. It was so easy like this. So right. Felicity should have been terrified, but she wasn't. She was on fire, and she was falling somewhere new, but she wasn't afraid at all.

Blair might have been surrounded by death,

but she carried so much life in her that Felicity couldn't run from her now. So she kissed her again, tasting lavender soap and the woods and Blair, Blair, Blair.

And it was enough to keep the ghosts at bay. For now.

Eleven

Harold Has a Friend

Blair had never seen Harold outside of the house before. Not until she glanced out the window after her bath and saw him chatting over a neatly trimmed hedge to an old, silver-haired woman — which was odd in itself. Harold didn't seem the type to chat, over hedges or anywhere else.

"Who's that? A guest?" If it was, Blair hadn't seen her before.

"Hmm?" Felicity hummed distractedly. She'd been in the middle of pinning her hair, but she tore away from the vanity mirror now to stand beside Blair. "Who?"

Blair pointed to Harold and the woman, tightening her bath towel closer to her chest and hoping nobody would walk past the window.

"Oh, that's Agnes. She's lived here longer than my grandfather has."

"How is that possible?"

Felicity shrugged and went back to her reflection. "I think she was eight or nine when he was born."

"But I mean... who is she?"

"The neighbor. The land past those hedges isn't ours. She has a little cottage on the other side of the fields."

"So..." Blair narrowed her eyes, cogs in her brain whirring to life again. "She'd know things, then? About Hartwell's history?"

As Blair turned, Felicity cast her a pointed look in the reflection, lips pursed knowingly. "You mean about my grandfather."

"Maybe," Blair sing-songed elusively, though of course they both knew that the answer was yes. Still, a new lead in an otherwise puzzling investigation gave Blair the energy to search for her clothes, remembering that Felicity had left them to dry on the radiator last night. She padded into the bathroom and came out a moment later with her arms in the wrong sleeves, the collar skew-whiff, and her stockings twisted all wrong.

"*Blair*." Felicity crossed her legs as though readying herself to give a lecture or else read a story. Blair suspected that, since there weren't many children's books in here, the former was more likely. "She's very old."

"I know. That's why I'd like to talk to her."

"You won't get much sense out of her. The last time I spoke to her, she was talking to her azaleas. A story about wicked fairies, I think."

"She sounds like somebody I'd get along perfectly well with, actually. Fairies *are* quite wicked sometimes."

Felicity regarded her skeptically, as though she couldn't quite tell if Blair was joking. These days, Blair couldn't, either. She buttoned her dress and tugged down the creased pleats. She was in dire need of an iron, but until she figured out who "T" was and why he was buried in the woods, it was low on her list of priorities.

"You don't have to come."

"Yes, I think I do." Felicity sighed and batted Blair's hands away so that she could wrestle with the stiff top button of her dress herself. Blair could only lower her hands, unsure when it had become so natural to be washing each other's hair and buttoning each other's clothes. They had only been together one night, and it hadn't quite been the blissful honeymoon period most couples spoke of, what with the sèance and ghost-led five o'clock venture into the forest this morning.

But here they were… and it wasn't strange, not for Blair. It was just strange that Felicity had been hiding so much beneath that cool facade. There was so much softness beneath those sharp edges. She had gone from despising Blair to whispering Blair's name into her mouth. Blair had been with both women and men before, never one to hold back on her desires or the liberation she so often protested for… but it had never felt with them as it had with Felicity last night. She had never slotted together with someone and felt that it was the right fit. The last person who *ever* should have fit was Felicity, and yet she had accepted Blair completely, kissed her all over, let her into her bed and perhaps even her heart.

And she hadn't run away in the morning. She'd run toward her. Had taken care of her. Blair had spent her strange little life alone save for the experiences shared with her mother. She never expected another person to make her feel supported. Normal, even. Felicity had no reason to. She hadn't even believed in the paranormal. But she'd provided Blair with a reassurance, a companionship, no one else ever had.

Blair would hold onto it until Felicity requested otherwise.

"You're staring at me," Felicity muttered, brows lowered in concentration.

"It's hard not to," Blair admitted gently. It was the truth. Anyone else might look at Felicity and think her plain, but Blair saw the pointed chin and the brown eyes and the pale face for what they were now: beautiful. Subtle and slightly strange, elfin, but beautiful. A bit like Hartwell Hall itself. A bit like everything Blair had ever loved. A bit like everything otherworldly.

Felicity's mouth quivered with a suppressed smile as she stepped away. "I have a Halloween party to organize for tomorrow night, so I'm going to be busy for the next couple of days, which means…."

What did it mean? That Felicity didn't want Blair hovering around her like a fly? "Which means?"

"It means I won't be able to see much of you during the day. And I was wondering if perhaps you might like to stay with me again tonight. Only in case the ghost comes back, of course. I wouldn't want you wandering barefoot into the woods again, is all."

"Of course. So it would merely be a precautionary measure." Blair smirked, inching forward and lacing her fingers through Felicity's.

"Exactly. A precaution." Felicity's nose brushed against Blair's cheek.

Blair couldn't hold back a moment longer. She pressed her lips to Felicity's, heat stirring in her stomach, down to her toes, and up to the crown of her head. They had surprised her, those lips: how soft they were, how willing. Felicity drew away first, but not without a final exploration across the seam of Blair's lips. And then she pressed her forehead against Blair's, breaths labored.

"Just another precaution?" Blair questioned.

"Well, one must always be cautious."

If Blair didn't leave the bedroom then, she might have stayed there with Felicity all day. So, with an awed giggle under her breath, Blair dragged Felicity out. They walked through the staff's quarters still holding hands, Blair's feet still stinging from all the thorns she'd stepped on.

Blair was sorry when, in the foyer, they finally had to let go.

Twelve

A Meeting with Agnes

Blair's stomach jittered with anticipation as she knocked on the door of Mulberry Cottage. She was close to unearthing all of this once and for all, and closer still now that she was here. Though the ghost was no longer holding her hand, she could feel his presence: more settled, less melancholy, light as a wispy cloud where it had once been a smothering torrent of hailstone.

Felicity stood beside her, inspecting the vegetable patch as though she was quite an avid fan of cabbages. Perhaps she was. Blair didn't know those things yet. More than likely, though, Felicity was trying to adjust to Blair's prying nature after a long time of being so reserved. They really did make quite an odd couple.

The door finally creaked open just as Blair was about to rap on it a second time, revealing the elderly woman who had been talking to Harold this morning. Her stark gray hair had fallen loose of its curlers, and her cheeks were hollow, but her pale eyes seemed friendly enough. A black cat dithered around her feet, watching Blair with about the same fiery hostility that Harold usually showed her.

"Hello, Agnes." Felicity stepped in front of Blair with a forced smile. "I'm not sure if you remember me. I'm Felicity Hartwell."

Agnes blinked blankly. "Harold's daughter?"

"Granddaughter, actually."

Her thin lips parted with shock, eyes widening. "By gum! I'd forgotten how old I was for a moment. Come in, come in! And bring your bonny little friend in with you, too!"

Blair didn't think anyone had ever called her "bonny" before and bit down on a smile as she followed Felicity into the cottage. Agnes had already wandered off down the shadowy hallway somewhere, so Blair shut the door, trying not to step on the belligerent cat in the process. Apparently, it had decided to guard the welcome mat, because it hissed at Blair when her shoe accidentally stepped onto it.

"Alright, alright, no need for that," she murmured incredulously, backing steadily away.

Felicity shot her a puzzled expression before heading through the first door on their left. A kitchen, Blair found, old-fashioned and lackluster. By the looks of the wonky cupboard doors and rusted hinges, the furniture had probably been here longer than Blair had been alive. She could certainly feel an awful lot of life swimming around these walls, though nothing distinct or in need of attention like Hartwell's ghost.

"Sit, sit, sit." Agnes motioned to the chairs set out around a small, round table littered with threads and needles. The tapestries hanging on every empty space of wallpaper showed the reason. From pigs to bible scriptures to tea towels embroidered with flowers, the kitchen was full of needlework. "I'll put the kettle on."

Blair followed Felicity in taking a seat, smiling politely as Agnes pottered around to fill the kettle and then heat it up on the stove. When she began muttering to herself, indistinguishable and nonsensical things that Blair couldn't make out, Felicity cast Blair a pointed look as though to say, "I told you so."

But Blair wasn't put off by it. She often talked to herself too, though she wouldn't admit it.

"I must admit, I don't get visitors very often these days," Agnes continued, setting out three teacups in chipped saucers with knobbly, unsteady fingers. "What did you say your friend is called? Margaret?"

Felicity frowned. "I hadn't introduced her yet. Her name is Blair, and she's a guest staying with us at Hartwell."

"Oh, how wonderful!" The corners of Agnes's eyes crinkled as she smiled. "I've always loved Hartwell and the lovely gardens you keep. Have you seen the gardens, Margaret?"

"I have. They're very lovely indeed." Blair shifted impatiently in her seat. Though Agnes and her affinity for gardens were certainly heartwarming, she hadn't come here to discuss the shrubs. It was for the same reason that she didn't correct her name a second time. "Have you lived here long, then, Miss Hastings?"

Agnes tutted. "Oh, please do call me Agnes." She had taken to stirring her spoon around her empty cup as though the tea had already been poured. Meanwhile, the kettle still bubbled on the stove. Perhaps she *was* a few shillings short of a pound after all — but that didn't mean she couldn't help. "Is that a Midlands accent I hear?"

Blair nodded. "I'm from Birmingham."

"Oh, how wonderful!" she repeated. Very few people would describe Blair's tired home city as such a thing, covered in coal dust and underpaid laborers still recovering from shellshock as it was.

The kettle screeched to the boil on the stove, and Agnes jumped out of her chair — surprisingly spritely for a woman who must have been pushing ninety. Blair had never met anybody who had lived past sixty, but she supposed people in the countryside, with clean air and leisurely lives, had a much greater chance of survival than the poverty-stricken families she was used to.

Turning the dial on the stove off, Agnes poured the water into a teapot and brought it over. Once everyone's cup was filled, Blair dropped a sugar cube and a splash of milk into hers, wondering how many cups of tea it would take before Agnes actually answered her question.

"You always did make the best cups of tea, Agnes," Felicity complimented, warming her hands around the cup. "Next time, I'll have to bring my granddad, Harold, around. You two always got along, didn't you?"

"Ah, yes, Harold. Such a quiet chap. Wouldn't buy any of my tomatoes, though I offered him a very generous discount. Would you like to try them?"

"Perhaps later," she declined politely. "We had quite a big breakfast."

"Felicity tells me the two of you are lifelong neighbors," Blair added, and then popped another sugar cube into her tea. It was awfully watery, and she would need it to get her through so many diversions of conversation. "How fascinating that must have been. Did you grow up together?"

"Of course! I remember when Harold was born, though I couldn't have been more than seven." Agnes pointed to something past Blair, and Blair craned her neck, peering out the window into the back garden. It was slightly overgrown, and Blair caught sight of the untamed tomato vines curling around a trellis. For a moment, Blair thought Agnes was about to offer out her tomatoes again, but instead, she said, "We used to play there on that tree there, or sometimes I would be allowed for tea at Hartwell and we'd run around the gardens playing hide and seek."

Indeed, a rope swing had been attached to a splintering branch of a large oak tree by the fence, and it swayed listlessly in the mild breeze now. Blair couldn't imagine Harold as a child playing there; his dark, brooding nature was so all-consuming, so endless, that Blair couldn't picture him any other way.

"What was my grandfather like as a child?" Felicity leaned forward in her chair, no longer here for Blair's suspicions but for an interest in a man she had both known and not known all her life.

"Oh, he was a lovely boy. He was always getting into trouble, mind, especially where his brother was involved."

Both of them stiffened at that. Blair's fingers tightened around the handle of her teacup until the delicate china threatened to shatter. "His brother?"

"Yes, little Timothy. Well, he was older than Harold, I think, but he was quite short, you see."

Timothy. Icy fingers crept down Blair's spine at the name — because she knew. It couldn't have been a coincidence. Timothy. "T." The young boy she had seen in Hartwell twice now was Harold's brother.

"My grandfather didn't have a brother." Felicity frowned. She hadn't put the pieces together yet, and Blair couldn't help her, not here, not in front of Agnes.

"Oh, but I remember him well." Agnes's papery features clouded. "I was awfully sorry to see him go when he moved away."

"Where did he go?" Blair had a feeling she already knew because he was still there now, still trapped, still calling for help.

"I can't quite remember. I think perhaps his mother might have said something about an aunt in London. He was such a bright boy. Probably got into one of those fancy boarding schools, did he?"

"Did you ever see him again?"

Agnes shook her head, perplexed. "Not that I can remember. Mind you, I can't remember what I had for breakfast these days. Did I tell you about my tomatoes? They're growing so marvelously, you know..."

Agnes began to ramble again, but this time, neither Blair nor Felicity was listening. Blair waited for Felicity to understand, waited for her to look at her. Finally, Felicity did, blinking rapidly as though it might make things clearer.

When Agnes excused herself to go and get her beloved tomatoes for them to try — she wouldn't be refused, no matter how much they both claimed to be stuffed from breakfast — Blair slipped her hand into Felicity's.

"I don't understand," Felicity whispered. She wouldn't meet Blair's gaze, and it made Blair think that perhaps she *did* understand but didn't yet want to.

"I think Harold did have a brother, Felicity, and I think he did go away — but not to boarding school."

Her features sharpened all at once, an echo of the woman she'd been when Blair had first met her. Cold and unforgiving and untrusting. It left Blair's palms clammy, anxiety twisting around her gut. She couldn't go back to this now. "What are you saying?"

"You know what I'm saying." Blair spoke softly, carefully, afraid that this might tear them apart — and so quickly after they had come together.

"No, I don't. And frankly, you'd be a fool to trust Agnes. She's old and senile, and she doesn't know half of what she's talking about."

Blair clenched her jaw, counted to five, and told herself to be patient, delicate, because this was new to Felicity and Blair wouldn't want to admit that somebody had disappeared in her family under mysterious circumstances, either. "I know this must be hard, Felicity, but it isn't a coincidence that Agnes says your grandfather's brother's name was Timothy while *I* have been seeing a boy with the same initial."

"Is it a coincidence that you're both ludicrously insane?"

There it was again. That bite. The condescension. The reminder that, no matter what they shared, Felicity was not like Blair and would always use that as a weapon when she had to face something she didn't want to.

Blair sucked in a deep breath and sat back in her chair, pain searing through her. She had told

Felicity about her past. About who she was and how she had come to be, laying herself bare both physically and emotionally. Perhaps it had been a mistake.

"So are we back to this?" Blair's voice echoed around the kitchen, as haunting as anything she had encountered of late.

Felicity bowed her head so that Blair could no longer gauge her expression and then cleared her throat. "No. No. But I'd *know* if my grandfather had a brother. I'd *know*." It sounded as though she was trying to convince herself more than Blair.

Sympathy welled in Blair, and she curled her hand around Felicity's again. "Would you? If something terrible happened… something that left a young boy's spirit trapped on your estate, nothing left of him but an unmarked grave in the woods… do you think Harold would tell you?"

Felicity chewed on her lower lip, remaining silent until she tore their hands apart and pushed away from the table to stand. "I need to talk to my father. I'll… I'll talk to you later."

"Felicity—"

But Felicity was gone, the front door slamming shut just a moment later, leaving the walls of the cottage to rattle in her wake. Agnes chose that same time to wander back into the kitchen, juggling a dozen large and wonkily shaped tomatoes in her arms.

"Oh, no. Felicity hasn't left, has she?" Her face fell in disappointment. "She didn't even try my tomatoes. Now we have six apiece."

Blair almost groaned.

∞∞∞

"Father...?" Felicity said, not for the first time that morning. In fact, she had been hovering around the front desk like a blue bottle in summer for an hour now and still had not mustered the courage to come out with it and ask him if he could confirm the wild conspiracies Agnes had given.

She didn't know what to make of it — any of it. Agnes was an old lady, away with the fairies. She could have conjured any sort of delusion regarding her childhood.

But Felicity couldn't deny that it *was* a coincidence that the two young boys from the past that Blair and Agnes had talked about both shared the same initial. It couldn't have meant anything. Because if it was true, if Timothy had existed and was now the spirit haunting Hartwell, the body beneath the unmarked grave... well, that would mean that Grandfather had either been witness to or part of something sinister. A cover-up of a child's death. A trauma Felicity couldn't even comprehend, mostly because she didn't want to.

"Yes?" Her father flicked through the guestbooks, brows furrowed distractedly. Maybe it was pointless. Maybe Father would know nothing about it. Maybe Felicity was just stalling. "Not in trouble again, am I? What now?"

She took a deep breath and shut the guestbook to draw his attention back to her. He looked up slowly, bewildered, his lips pursed into a fine line bracketed by aging and a small cut he must have made while shaving this morning.

"What is it?" He was here with her now. Listening.

"I have a strange question for you."

"Oh, bloody hell. Mr. Kane hasn't been asking what's in the black puddings again, has he?"

"No." Though Felicity didn't blame Mr. Kane for the concern in that regard. "No. It's nothing to do with the guests."

"Then what?" Father straightened up until he was his usual head taller than Felicity.

"Well, I was wondering... *well...*" *Oh, for heaven's sake, spit it out*, she scolded herself. "Did Grandfather have any siblings?"

His dark eyes turned quizzical, his fingers inching back to the guestbook as though the question had never warranted it being closed. "No. No, he was an only child. Why?"

"I was talking to Agnes. She seems to remember another boy growing up with her and Granddad. A brother named Timothy."

"Are you sure it wasn't *her* brother?" he questioned. "The old woman has lost a fair few of her marbles in her old age."

"No. She remembers Granddad's brother, Timothy. Apparently, he went to boarding school in London and she never saw him again."

Father chewed the lid of his pen pensively. "You know, come to think of it, we *have* been hiding a great uncle from you. We were going to tell you on your thirtieth birthday, but you've found us out now. The surprise is ruined."

Felicity's face remained deadpan, unimpressed. "Sarcasm is the lowest form of wit."

"I don't know, Felicity. Agnes has clearly gotten her wires crossed." He pointed his pen at her accusingly then. "And don't you dare pester Granddad about this. We've only just recovered from last night's explosion."

Felicity had no intentions of doing such a thing to begin with. She'd rather spend the rest of her life not knowing than have to face Granddad and his bad temper. Blair, on the other hand, would probably not be put off if the man started spitting out fire like a dragon.

Speaking of the devil, the front doors rattled with a visitor — and it was Blair who stepped into the foyer, cheeks puffed out as though she was about to retch. "I have just eaten six tomatoes. *Six*. Big ones, too."

Felicity winced apologetically. She shouldn't have left Blair alone with Agnes, but she had been so confused and still was.

"Dare I ask why?" Father replied, glancing warily at Blair.

"Agnes," she and Felicity explained at the same time.

"Hang on. You were there, too? Why?"

Unsure how to reply without telling her father about everything else she'd discovered recently, Felicity only shifted and looked to Blair for guidance. She supposed a man should know if there was a mysterious boy buried on his grounds — *if* that was the case. But telling him would mean admitting that he'd been right about the haunted house nonsense the whole time, for starters. And then there was the matter of unearthing family secrets that Felicity wasn't sure she wanted to unearth.

Blair's eyes darted from Felicity and back again. Subtly, Felicity shook her head.

"Er... I'm just very fond of tomatoes, so I asked Felicity if I could join her," Blair said finally.

Hopeless. Felicity's eyes fluttered closed. At least now she knew for certain that Blair wasn't a charlatan. She clearly couldn't lie to save her life.

Father remained unconvinced. "Then it has nothing to do with the investigation I'm *paying* you to carry out?"

"Alright, fine. The tomatoes were awful. I hid three of them in my dress." Blair tugged at the collar of her dress and drew out the three tomatoes in question, leaving Father to flush the exact same shade of red as the fruit. The man wasn't used to such... immodesty, Felicity supposed. They both eyed the tomatoes warily when she left them on the desk. "I went to Agnes to ask a few questions about... well, your family history. So yes, it is part of the investigation."

"So…" Curiosity played across Father's features, his focus flickering between Blair and Felicity like a pendulum clock. Felicity tried to keep her features as neutral as she could; tried not to show what felt to be written all over her: that she and Blair were something they were not supposed to be. "Felicity. You're working on this investigation too, are you?"

"I wouldn't go that far. I'm… assisting when necessary."

A line formed between Dad's brows, smug pride twitching across his lips. "What an interesting turn of events. My daughter, a skeptic, assisting a paranormal investigator."

"You won't be happy when you hear what we've found." Felicity supposed that there was no avoiding it now. It was he who had wanted this investigation to begin with.

He surveyed the foyer for any loitering guests. Even upon finding it empty, he motioned them both closer — and rightly so. Business would probably dwindle a little bit if the guests caught wind of a corpse buried on the estate. "Then was I right? Is it a ghost?"

The question was aimed at Blair, and she nodded solemnly in response, hands clasped together tightly. "I'm afraid so. Sometimes, a spirit might linger in one place after their passing, particularly if they have unfinished business."

"But what has that to do with my imaginary

Uncle Timothy?"

"The spirit is a boy," Blair whispered, and it left Felicity's arms covered in goosebumps beneath the sleeves of her dress. "His presence is strongest in the old playroom. That's where I saw him for the first time."

Felicity watched the color drain from Father's face as Blair continued.

"He showed me something. A letter 'T' drawn behind the wallpaper in room eleven. It must be his first initial. We didn't know much more about him until... until we found a small grave in the middle of the woods this morning. It was carved with the same letter. It must be where he's buried."

Father began to tremble: his jaw, his hands, his entire being. His throat bobbed against his bow tie. "I don't understand...."

"And then I saw Agnes speaking with your father this morning," Blair said as though he hadn't spoken at all. "Felicity told me that they grew up together, and with the way Harold has responded to my presence and my questions, I'm certain he knows more than he's letting on. So I decided to test the theory. I asked Agnes about her childhood, and she told me she remembers Harold's brother. A boy named Timothy. Allegedly, he went off to boarding school in London and she never saw him again.

"Only I don't think he went to boarding school, Mr. Hartwell. I think that he was killed and buried in those woods. I don't know how or why or by who. I'm not accusing your family of anything unseemly. I just… I don't think it's a coincidence that everything links together. I can't imagine how you must feel after this news. If you wish to separate yourself from your investigation, I understand, but I can't walk away now. I have to find out the truth and help the boy pass on."

Moments of silence passed, the grandfather clock ticking in the corner to count the seconds for them. And then Father cleared his throat, pinched his earlobe, and straightened his bow tie. His gaze turned back to Felicity. "And you have seen the grave, too?"

"Yes," she whispered hoarsely. "I don't know if I believe Agnes and her tales about Granddad, but I do know that there are things happening in this place that shouldn't be, and Blair seems to be the only one able to help."

A nod. "I can't pretend as though I know everything about my father. He's always been a reserved man, and I seldom felt close to him growing up. If Timothy existed, Dad never told me, and I'm not sure we can use Agnes as a reliable source."

"Which is why I need proof," Blair said. "Do you perhaps have old records? Birth certificates, photographs, diaries? Anything that might date back to Harold's childhood?"

"If we do, I couldn't tell you where." He scratched at his chin uncertainly. "Should we alert somebody about… the grave?"

"Not yet. I need to find out the truth myself first so that I can help the boy. If the authorities start sniffing around, it could get in the way. They're not usually ones to step back and let a paranormal investigator solve their cases for them."

And they would chase away all the guests, Felicity almost added, but she knew it was selfish and despised herself for even thinking it. "Then we carry on as we are," she said instead. "Blair has done a good job of finding the truth so far, and we can help where we can."

They all nodded, uneasy, both the closest people Felicity had in her world and yet strangers in this moment. Everything was different, foreign. Everything had changed. The patterning on the walls was not the shade of brown she remembered; the chandelier seemed to cast eerie, prismed light that floated along the staircase; even her father was different, more determined, square-jawed and shouldered. This was not the place she had grown up in. This was not the safe home she knew. This was a place of ghosts and secrets.

But in the middle of it all was Blair, and Felicity trusted that she would make things right. She would have to. Otherwise, Felicity would spend the rest of her life haunted, and she refused to let that happen.

Thirteen

A New Lead

It was Nancy who helped Blair sneak into Harold's rooms. Unlike Felicity, he stayed on the top floor with the entire east corridor to himself; one room was his bedroom, the other a study. Blair hadn't told Felicity about it — the less she knew, the better. She wouldn't be best pleased if she was dragged into another confrontation with her grandfather, and Blair only needed to find some evidence that Timothy had existed in Harold's childhood.

So when Harold went downstairs for his roast dinner that evening, Nancy led Blair into Harold's study under the guise of cleaning his rooms — which, to be fair, wasn't actually a guise. Nancy dusted the bookshelves and polished the mantel while Blair rooted through drawers upon drawers of paperwork that were not even a little bit exciting.

It was dark up here too, even with the sun

not yet set completely, as though any light simply refracted away from this corner of the house.

"Found anything?" Nancy asked as she moved onto neatening up the desk.

Blair was knelt on the floor still, bored witless while skimming through bills and old newspaper clippings about horse racing results. "Not a thing. The man is very dull." Even the books on the shelves were all nonfiction.

"Perhaps you'll have better luck in the bedroom."

Blair agreed, and the two creeped back out to the corridor and into Harold's bedroom.

It was just as drab as his study, which accounted for the books he'd possessed on minimalism, Blair supposed. His bed was already made with plain gray sheets, and that was about the only splash of color in here other than a cup of tea left out on the bedside table.

"Are we sure Harold isn't an automaton?" Blair muttered, beginning her search with the trunk at the bottom of the bed. Inside, she found only bedsheets and striped pajamas. It was as though the man was new to the world; there were no signs that he'd ever played an active part in his existence. The books on his bedside tables were untouched, the spines not even a little bit creased. The lenses of the reading spectacles beside them were free of any smudges. The drawers were empty save for the ones in the dresser, which Blair opened and promptly shut again upon discovering undergarments. No ghost or mystery would have her rooting through an old man's briefs.

She'd almost given up when her clumsy hands knocked a bottle of cologne to the floor. She winced against the bang, thankful that it at least didn't shatter or spill. Nancy whirled around to see what the commotion was about, her duster's feathers molting along the floor.

"Oops," Blair whispered, crouching to pick it up. The tattered corner of a brown leather spine stopped her in her tracks, poking out just slightly from the shadows beneath Harold's bed.

Curiosity was a beast roused from slumber, and it had made its bed in Blair's gut. She abandoned the cologne, leaving it rolling on the floorboards, forgotten. Her only focus now was this book, this one solitary book, left concealed and scuffed where the others had been in piles, untouched.

Because it wasn't just a book, Blair found as she slid it out slowly. It was unlabeled, and inside were pages upon pages of creased, ink-stained paper and scrawled, spiky handwriting with dates and dreams and memories. Blair flipped to where the string had been left toward the end of the book first, her heart beginning to stutter in her chest.

Yesterday's date was at the top of the page: a diary entry. Beneath, a list.

11:03 a.m.
Creaking in the attic.

1:16 p.m.
Flattened grass again. Wasn't like that this morning.
3:45 p.m.
Mrs. Walters says her son has lost another toy. Pedal car. Hasn't found it yet.
5:37 p.m.
Shadow on the edge of the woods.
11 p.m.
More dreams. This time, it's me who falls. Woke up shivering. Think he was in my room again.

The jotted sentences made no sense to Blair, and yet still they left a shiver dancing through her bones all the same. From what she could gather, they were records of sightings and traces of Timothy, just like the sort Blair had been keeping. Her eyes kept snagging on the last part, though. The only instance where the author referred to himself.

This time, it's me who falls.

Is that what had happened to Timothy? Had he fallen somewhere? Or perhaps it was a metaphor, a recurring nightmare of an event that had become distorted over the years. Blair could be sure of nothing. She flicked back to the first page, examining the dates as she went.

1914. An entry about Vincent going off to war.

1901. A birthday.

House has been quiet recently. Has he finally gone?

And there was his wife's death, from what Blair could gather, solemn enough that tears sprang to her eyes. That was 1899.

Will she haunt me, too?

1897. Felicity's birth.

House went cold when they brought her home. What must he think of the new lives?

Sometimes the entries trailed off for a while. There was a year's gap between 1888 and 1889. A three-year gap from 1870 to 1873. But they always came back. *He* always came back, with new experiences, new reports. A whispering in his ear, a teapot knocked from a shelf, a hand around his wrist. And Blair saw Timothy in them: She saw him as he was now, desperate to be free; she saw him angry, causing havoc for Harold and the guests; she saw him lonely, taking children's toys, leaving the playroom in pieces. A child sworn never to grow up.

But she also saw Harold in these pages, in a way she hadn't been able to when they spoke face to face. He was tired. A tired old man confined to a life of being haunted. Bitter, sometimes. ("Why won't he leave me?") Accepting, others. ("Candle extinguished tonight on its own. Saying goodnight?")

Always haunted. Always followed by Timothy.

The entries began in 1859 with the scruffy hand of a young boy, but even then, there was nothing to suggest the experiences were new. Sixty-four years, Harold had kept this diary. Blair couldn't comprehend a life like that, and she had had a fair few experiences with the dearly departed herself. Sympathy welled in her, and she wasn't sure if it was for Timothy or Harold. They were both trapped here, both tethered by something that had happened. Something to do with the fall.

The word "attic" seemed to pop out from the scribbles again and again, though. "Creaking in the attic." "Screams in the attic." "Vincent thinks there are squirrels in the attic." Blair thought of the pull she had felt to that square shaft in the ceiling above her room, and she knew she had to find a way up there.

"Nancy?" Her voice rang like metal against metal in her own ears, breaking the thick silence.

"Hmm?" Nancy was fluffing the pillows and straightening out the duvet. She hadn't noticed Blair's discovery at all.

"Do you perchance know where I might find a stepladder?"

Nancy stopped over the bed and frowned. "I'm sure there are some in one of the storage closets, but whatever do you need them for?"

"I need to go up to the attic." Blair waved the notebook around, a cocktail of sweet excitement and acidic dread swirling in her. She was closer than ever, and she could feel the fact washing over her like a warm gust of wind on a summer's day. "I think I may have found something important."

"Oh, dear lord, is that a diary?"

"I know, I know." Blair pushed the diary back under the bed where she'd found it and then stood to brush the lint from her dress. "I'm a rotten snoop. But I was right, Nancy. Harold is the key to all this. He's been monitoring the ghost since 1859, and he talks about Timothy as though he knows him — *knew* him — personally."

Nancy lifted her brows, teeth sinking into her lower lip. "Nobody has been up to the attic in years. Is it safe?"

Blair only shrugged, determination glittering in her eyes along with the disrupted dust. "There's only one way to find out."

Fourteen

Ghost in the Attic

The rules, as set by Felicity after Blair told her about the notebook, were that Blair must wait until the Halloween party, when no guests or staff members would be around to see her climbing her way into the attic. Of course, Felicity had expected Blair to at least stop by the taproom for a drink first and was rather disappointed when she didn't. She had put on one of her favorite black dresses tonight, velvety and sequined and matched with gloves. And because she had thought Blair might like it, she'd even painted her lips a deep crimson and dabbed a little shadow and mascara around her eyes. Felicity didn't usually dress up for Halloween, even at her own parties, but she'd wanted to this year. Had thought that perhaps Blair might want to, too.

But she should have known that Blair was too rapt in the investigation for anything else now. Besides, they had shared a bed again last night, among other things. It wasn't as though Blair had stopped paying interest in Felicity altogether.

Still, the dress deserved to be seen, so Felicity waited until all of the guests had guzzled at least one round of drinks and Mrs. Walters had already pushed chairs aside to dance wildly before she slipped away into the shadows.

The rest of Hartwell was dead as the leaves outside tonight, and Felicity's heels seemed louder than ever as they clicked across the tiles of the foyer and up the stairs to the top floor. It was not surprising in the least when she found Blair balancing precariously on a set of stepladders in the west wing, dress riding up to her stocking-covered thighs as she attempted to unlatch the attic door.

"Don't fall," Felicity warned after watching in amusement for a few moments.

Blair almost toppled from the ladders, startled as she was, her knuckles turning white as she gripped a rung and peered through the slats to see who had disturbed her. Her alarm dissipated when she found Felicity, though she remained slightly pale, and Felicity almost felt guilty. Almost.

She sighed and planted her foot on the lowest rung instead so that the ladders were a little sturdier against the uneven carpets. "You couldn't have waited for me to help?"

"I didn't want to take you from your party." Blair's voice came out strained as she stretched up to the hatch again. "You look lovely, by the way. Less scary than usual, actually, which seems backwards for Halloween."

Felicity pursed her lips, unsure whether that could be considered a compliment. "And you aren't dressed up at all."

"I am. I'm dressed up as a paranormal investigator about to solve a very strange mystery to help a ghost pass on to whatever awaits in the next life. It's not my fault that I dress like that every other day, too."

It was a fair point, and one that was followed by the splintering sound of the attic door opening. It swung on rusted hinges, bringing with it dangling cobwebs and dust and an awful, unsettling dank smell that reminded Felicity of her night in the basement not so long ago. Anxiety fluttered with sharp-edged wings in her gut, but she paid it no heed when Blair smiled down at her and began to climb up the ladder to the highest step.

The rungs rattled under Felicity's foot as Blair pushed off and became nothing more than a set of dangling legs before disappearing into the blackness completely.

Felicity supposed that the latch remaining open was the only invitation she was to get and made her own cautious way up, too. When she reached the attic floor, head submerged in shadows, she found Blair standing over her, arms extended to help. Felicity took them and crawled up, rotting wood sinking under her feet. And then Blair pulled up the latch and there was nothing.

Not for a moment, anyway. Then Blair

sneezed, almost frightening the life out of her. Felicity's eyes adjusted soon after, and she caught a patch of cloudy moonlight slipping in through the angled window above. "I don't suppose you brought a torch."

Blair patted herself down as though it might be hidden in a nonexistent pocket. "I suppose with my line of work, I really should start carrying one."

Felicity rolled her eyes and finally dared a glance around. The attic was as awful as she'd imagined, a few dusty, crumbling tables and chairs gathering enough cobwebs to spin a dress from. When she quieted her breathing, she was certain she could hear something scuttling nearby — so she did not quiet her breathing. If there were rats or spiders or other forsaken creatures around her feet, she'd rather not know about them.

Too eagerly, Blair moved ahead of her to examine the things that had been abandoned over the years: cardboard boxes with old lamps, pillows with mold that would never wash out, old guestbooks that probably dated back to years before Felicity had even existed.

"What are you hoping to find?" asked Felicity, trying not to shiver as she passed across a shaft of cold air.

Blair crouched among piles of old books and envelopes, hands tracing slowly across their surfaces. "I think perhaps I've already found it."

∞∞∞

It was a photograph. Faded and difficult to make out in the light, but it was what Blair had needed. Her fingers traced along the silver plate, the protective glass miraculously unshattered. She couldn't quite believe it was real, somehow. Everything she had been searching for, every bit of proof — it was in the photograph and the young, familiar face at the center of it.

"What is it?" Felicity asked, hovering over Blair's shoulder, as light-footed as a spirit herself.

"A family portrait," Blair whispered. "Do you know any of them?"

Felicity joined Blair on the floor, her warmth curling around Blair's body. It was a comfort to have her here. A comfort not to have to sit in the darkness alone this time, as she had so often before.

She heard Felicity's breath hitch, heard her breaths become shallow as she examined the picture. "The younger boy… he looks so much like my father."

But it wasn't Vincent, Blair knew. It could only have been Harold.

"And the parents," Felicity continued. "I've only seen them in a few paintings before, but I'm certain they're my great-grandparents." And then she gasped, fingers pale and stark in the shadows rising to her mouth. "Oh, my goodness. The other boy...."

"It's the boy I saw," Blair finished quietly, unexplained tears pricking at her eyes. She could no longer blame it on the dust. "Timothy."

"Then it's true. My grandfather did have a brother."

"And now Harold is haunted by him."

Outside, the wind rattled as though confirming her words, and with it the window above them, just slightly loose from its latch, so that a draught sent the papers on the floor flapping.

Blair stood up, heart rising to her throat and tightening there like two hands. There were steps beneath the window. Behind the glass pane, slicing through the moonlight, a shadow waited.

It moved too quickly for Blair to make it out, but it was there. A smudge in her periphery, a hint, a guide she was supposed to follow. She could feel him again now, tugging her along by invisible rope, toward the window. There was something there he wanted her to see.

"Blair?"

Blair barely heard Felicity's voice. She was too busy freeing the latch and opening the window. When she touched the cold metal, she felt other hands too, from memories that weren't hers. "They used to come up here."

"Who?"

"Harold and Timothy." She didn't know how she knew, only that she did. They had been here, had left their fingerprints seared into the world, and if they were a trail, it ended up there, on the roof.

Blair rose onto the first step.

"Blair," Felicity repeated, closer now. The wind was already whipping through Blair's hair, stealing her breath, freezing her skin. "Don't go out there. It's not safe."

But she had to. She had to if she wanted to finally learn what had happened to the little boy who had disappeared. She took another step.

"*Blair!*"

It was too late. She rose onto the roof, the wind tearing through her dress, her skin. A faint scream rent through the night, and she inched forward, toward the low parapet, the final barrier between her and the ground.

She could imagine it. Two boys playing in the attic. Finding out they could get onto the roof. Exhilarated, as tall as the birds and the trees and Hartwell itself. How wonderful it must have been. How terrible.

Another scream and a hand guiding her forward, just like the night she'd found the grave. Timothy, making sure Blair finished her job tonight. The gardens became visible at the edge of the roof, so far away. A whisper of the taproom's upbeat music drifted from the ground floor, strips of golden light pouring out onto the grass. Nobody knew she was up here.

Had anybody known he was? Had Harold?

"Blair, come down!"

Blair hated the raw, wavering terror in Felicity's voice, but there was nothing she could say or do with that hand in hers again. It slipped into her palm as though it was the most natural thing in the world. He led her to the parapet, drew her to the stone. It wanted her to touch.

So she did.

It flashed before her all at once: piercing screams; a shove against a fragile spine; the feeling of flying, falling, breath clawed from lungs, and ground stolen from grappling feet and then returned too hard, too fast, to survive such sudden impact.

He was pushed. Timothy was pushed.

Blair didn't realize she was sobbing until the jagged sounds cracked through the vision, nor did she realize that she was too close to the edge herself, leaning forward, forward, forward—

"Blair!" The scream pierced her eardrums, and then warm arms wrapped around her and tugged her back until she stumbled. Felicity's face was tear-stricken and bone white, body heaving with cries. "What were you doing? You could have fallen!"

"He had to show me," Blair mumbled, not sure if anything she was saying was the least bit coherent. She was both numb and not. Unreachable and yet somehow able to feel everything: every guttering star and every fiber of Felicity's dress bunched in her hands, every tear rolling down her cheek, and every hum along the wind. "He had to show me what happened."

Felicity's face crumpled with confusion. Her lips parted, but nothing came out save a mangled sound of disapproval.

"He was *pushed*, Felicity. He was pushed from this roof. Here. This is where he died. He was so young...."

Pain opened up like a chasm in Blair's chest, threatening to swallow everything around her. She didn't want to feel it anymore. She didn't want to know. She tried to push it away, but it wouldn't leave her, and all she had to hold onto as she continued to fall was Felicity.

She grasped on for dear life as Felicity pulled her to her chest, trembling and yet the most solid thing Blair had ever known. Keeping her together, whole, and here. She had never lost herself so deeply before now, never risked her life to figure out the end of somebody else's, but Felicity had kept her from the same fate Timothy had suffered tonight.

"I'm sorry," she whispered, teeth chattering. "I didn't mean to scare you."

Felicity shushed her, rocking her back and forth just slightly. "You're okay now. I wouldn't let you fall."

But Blair was falling. In so many ways, she was falling. And she wondered if perhaps — *hoped* — Felicity was falling too, so she searched for her lips to find out, to feel again, to anchor herself back to the present; she found them salty with tears. They clung onto each other with desperate hands and kissed the shadows away, and Blair was here, safe, and so was Felicity, and it was enough just for a moment until she could catch her breath.

When she pulled away, though, the shadows still lingered in the cobwebbed corners. She wasn't finished yet. Timothy still needed her. He was still trapped.

"It was Harold who pushed him." She hadn't seen his face, but she knew. There was no other reason why Timothy still lingered. No other reason why Harold was the way he was, why he had written all of those guilt-soaked words in his diary. *This time, it's me who falls.* "We have to find him."

Speechless, Felicity could only nod. They stayed there, though, until it was too cold to stand, clinging onto one another as though their skin might meld together if they just remained close enough.

Blair looked out to the gardens just once more, mourning a boy she had never known — and froze. Against the gray landscaping, a shadow was wending its way down toward the woods, tall and round. "Felicity."

Felicity stiffened against her and followed her gaze, frowning. "That isn't the same shadow I saw the other night."

"No." But they were heading into the same part of the woods as Blair had staggered into yesterday morning. Toward the grave. She had a feeling she might know who this one was. "It's someone else. A man with a guilty conscience paying his respects to the dead, perhaps."

There was nothing to do but find out.

Fifteen

Laid to Rest

Felicity was still trembling when she and Blair walked into the forest hand in hand. It didn't help that there was little to light their way. The waning full moon had been concealed by black clouds, casting nothing more than a faint, eerie silver glow that never quite reached them beyond the trees.

She couldn't think of what waited for them. It was too much to consider: her grandfather, a murderer. He had always been cold, distant, but Felicity had just thought it a product of the times in which he'd been born. That, and her father had always claimed that Grandfather had been raised by quite odd parents. Pious and severe. Enough to make any man a little bit unsociable.

Part of Felicity wanted to believe that Blair was wrong. That the shadow they'd seen entering the forest had been an illusion born from the distress they'd faced together on the roof or else a drunken guest who had wandered from the party. But when they reached the grave, the shadow was there. She knew that drooping set of shoulders hunched before the makeshift headstone and could no longer find an easier explanation for the truth.

This was the truth. Her grandfather had had a brother, and he had died falling from the roof of Hartwell Hall.

If Grandfather heard them approach, he didn't show it, though they had not attempted to hide their footsteps and the twigs splintered under their feet. He was too still, as though he was a silhouetted statue.

It was, of course, Blair who was the one brave enough to speak first.

"Mr. Hartwell?" Her voice fell softer than perhaps Grandfather deserved, and she let go of Felicity's hand to inch forward slightly.

Grandfather whipped around, eyes wide but glassy. Somewhere else. Now Felicity thought of it, perhaps he had always been somewhere else.

His usual cruel features were slack, hollow, his face drained of color. "What on earth are the two of you doing here? Get back to the party. It isn't safe for young ladies to be out at night."

"Granddad," Felicity uttered softly, and then wasn't sure what else she could say. They had to tread this line carefully. Grandfather wasn't prone to calm conversation, and nothing would be resolved if they triggered his anger. "We'd like to talk to you."

"Not now. Tomorrow." Weariness made his voice feeble. For whatever reason, something about tonight had weakened his spirit, dampened his flames. Did he already know that they'd found out the truth?

"Mr. Hartwell, there's a boy here who is trapped." Blair dared another step forward, wringing her hands until they turned white. "A young spirit, unable to pass through the veil peacefully. His name is Timothy... but you knew that already, didn't you?"

"How *dare* you?" Grandfather rose from his haunches, lips twisting with bitterness. For Blair or for himself? "Get away. Now. Go back to the party."

Blair shook her head, regret clouding her features. "I'm afraid I can't do that. You see, Mr. Hartwell, I came here to help... but the only person who can truly help now is you."

He tilted his chin stubbornly, but Felicity saw the way it wobbled, leaving his jowls and his shoulders wobbling, too. A man unraveling at the seams. "I don't know what you mean."

"Yes, you do," Blair said. "And you can't run away from this any longer."

Her eyes slid to something past Grandfather, her lips parting in a surprise that she attempted to hide quickly. But Felicity had seen it, and she followed her gaze. Her own breath caught in her throat at what she found, hairs prickling across every inch of her skin.

A boy. Timothy. Just as he'd been in the photographs, wearing creased shorts and uneven knee-high socks with a blazer that didn't quite fit his skinny frame yet. He stood behind the grave, expression somber and mousy-brown curls falling into his eyes.

Grandfather hadn't noticed him yet, his steely focus still locked on Blair. "I've been running for far longer than you can imagine, girl. I can manage a few more years."

"How long has it been?" Felicity couldn't help but ask, voice wavering as she forced her attention from Timothy.

Without pause to think, without so much as a beat, Grandfather replied, "Sixty-five years, this time. Sixty-five years today."

"That's a long time to spend being haunted, Mr. Hartwell," Blair whispered. "Isn't it time to let him go?"

"Let him go?" he spat vehemently. "You have no idea what you're talking about. You don't let go of what happened — of what I did. There *is* no letting go."

Blair seemed to soften, and Felicity wondered what it was she felt that Felicity didn't — how she could look her grandfather in the eye and speak so calmly, so sympathetically, after what he'd done. "That's not true. He's been trying to contact you all this time. You haven't wanted to listen."

"I listened!" Spittle flew from his mouth, eyes blazing with fierce madness. "I've been listening! I've paid my dues! I've lived with him and his punishments every day for sixty-five years!"

Behind Grandfather, Timothy shook his head. Blair watched and then murmured, "No... no, that's not what it was, was it? They weren't punishments."

Another shake of Timothy's head.

"Timothy was never a malevolent spirit, Mr. Hartwell. He wasn't here to harm you."

"Then why?" The question rattled in Grandfather's chest, desperate and hopeless and... *afraid*.

"Because... because it was an accident, wasn't it?"

Felicity frowned. An accident? But Blair said that Timothy had been pushed. How could it ever have been an accident?

But Timothy was nodding. Confirming.

"Of course, it was. Of course, it was a bloody accident. I never meant..." Grandfather choked on his own words, on a thick sob. It rattled something deep in Felicity. She had never seen her grandfather so much as laugh, let alone *cry*. "We were playing. We got too giddy, going up on the roof like that. Boys get that way, don't they? They get rough with each other. I hadn't realized he was so close to the edge... I hadn't...."

The pain in his voice left Felicity feeling raw, and she squeezed her eyes closed, her own tears burning through her lids. It was an accident. A mistake. Felicity remembered plenty of them growing up with Arthur. She still felt guilty when she thought of the scar in the corner of his brow, caused by falling out of a tree she had dared him to climb. She could only imagine what it must have been like to cause a death. To cause your brother's death.

"But if it was an accident, why is he buried here?" Felicity questioned. "Why was it hidden?"

"I begged my parents to call for a doctor. I *screamed*. But they said he was dead, that I'd killed him. They were cold people, just like the rest of this forsaken family. They didn't want Hartwell's good reputation to be marred by a family death. That's all that mattered: the money. The business. We were just children getting in the way with our silly games. 'You should be seen, not heard,' they always said. Well, after that, we were neither. I hid myself away, and Timothy…" Another heart-wrenching choke, another step towards breaking. "Timothy was gone."

"It wasn't your fault," Blair said.

Grandfather's gaze snapped upward, steely as the sharpened edge of a butcher's knife. "I *killed* him."

"By accident. You made a mistake, Mr. Hartwell, but you're not a murderer. And all of Timothy's attempts to contact you through the years… they weren't punishments. He only wanted to tell you that you were forgiven."

Blair was so close to Felicity's grandfather that she could have reached out and touched his shoulder, and Felicity found herself wondering if she might. But they stayed still as stone, Blair taller than him in his hunched state. Felicity could only wonder where she got her strength. Her own heart was breaking, and it was an effort not to collapse for the boy who had died and the other who had had to live without him.

"In my line of work," Blair continued steadily, "I often find that spirits linger and show us signs because they have unfinished business. All this time, I thought that Timothy wanted me to find his killer, but he didn't, not really. His unfinished business wasn't vengeance for his death or even justice. It was because he knew you still suffered without him. He stayed because he can't pass on without you knowing that he forgave you — and that you must forgive yourself."

"How?" Grandfather looked as lost as the boy behind him, still standing, watching, letting Blair deliver the words he couldn't say.

"Look behind you, Mr. Hartwell," Blair whispered.

He frowned for a moment, confused, and then turned slowly. Blair backed away as he did, her hand finding Felicity's again. It was warm in this abyss of darkness and frost, and Felicity held onto with every bit of strength she had left as she watched shock settle on her grandfather's face.

And Timothy... Timothy smiled. He had

been waiting all this time to be seen, and now he was.

Grandfather lifted a quaking hand to his mouth. "Tim."

"Harry," Timothy replied, familiarity and affection fringing his tone. He was still so child-like for a boy who had been here longer than Felicity had. "You are silly, waiting all this time to say goodbye."

"I was afraid. I thought you hated me."

Shadows danced in Timothy's eyes, and he shoved his hands into the pockets of his shorts as though it was the most natural conversation on earth. "I could never hate you. You're my brother. You only wanted to play, didn't you?"

"Of course. Of course, I did. I would never want to hurt you. I never meant…."

"I know. It was an accident. So why can't you let me go, Harry?"

"Because… because you'll fall." Grandfather's voice was nothing more than a rasp, as muted as the crisp wind whistling through the tree branches. The words were another crack in Felicity's beaten heart. Grandfather was still reliving that night, still reaching out to catch his brother. "You'll leave me alone."

"You're not alone. Neither am I." Timothy's eyes slid to Blair and Felicity, a fondness twinkling in them. Felicity saw the likeness to the rest of her family, but more than that, she saw life, too. Whatever doubts she'd had of the paranormal, of ghosts, of life after death, they all diminished with that smile. This boy was real, and he was here with the rest of them. Felicity had been a fool to ignore the signs for so long.

Grandfather glanced over his shoulder at them both too, awe leaving him gaping.

"Nobody here blames you, Mr. Hartwell," Blair said. "You're forgiven. Now you have to forgive yourself — for you and your brother."

He turned back to Timothy, white hair glinting off a ray of moonlight that had strayed from the clouds. "You forgive me?"

Timothy blinked sincerely. "I never had to forgive you, Harry. We're just silly children, after all, and silly children always make mistakes."

Grandfather nodded, slowly first and then so fast his head might have fallen from his neck. "Yes. Yes, we were."

"There we go, then." Timothy flashed a toothy grin that almost set Felicity laughing. Almost. "It's past bedtime now, so I'd better be off. You'll be alright without me, won't you, Harry?"

Another nod and then a watery chuckle. "Yes, Timmy. I'll be alright. Perhaps... perhaps I'll see you again one day soon."

"'Night, then." He waved at them all and then ambled away from the grave, deeper into the forest, a gray figure retreating into nothingness.

And then he became part of that nothing too, disappearing all at once until Felicity squinted to find him.

She understood too late that she wouldn't. Timothy was gone. He'd passed on, just as he'd wanted. The only thing keeping him here — Grandfather's guilt — was no longer anchoring him into Hartwell's soil.

Grandfather turned around, and Felicity found his cheeks streaked with tears. But his frame seemed straighter, his shoulders no longer caving in with the weight of his pain. Timothy had been freed tonight, but perhaps so had he.

And Felicity could think of nothing better to say or do than to go to her grandfather and wrap her arms around him. He swayed against her for a moment and then returned the embrace, the two of them treading this foreign territory together in an awkward but not unwelcome joining.

"You can let go now, Granddad," Felicity whispered. "You can let go."

He didn't let go: not to Felicity, not for a long while. But when they made their way back to Hartwell, Felicity could see that the shadows in his eyes and around his neck had eased, his brown eyes brighter than she'd ever known them to be.

He had let go. He could rest easy tonight without being haunted. They all could.

Sixteen

The Calm After the Storm

It was never discussed that Blair would sleep with Felicity again tonight. After seeing Harold off at the stairs, Felicity dragged Blair into the staff's quarters without asking, and only when they were in her room with the candles and lamps lit could Blair breathe again.

It had taken it out of Blair tonight. The almost falling from a roof, and then the finding a way for Harold to forgive himself. Her visions had never been so strong before, her connection to the dead never so real. She didn't yet know if Timothy was the cause or the house or Blair finally coming to appreciate her talents for what they were: a gift. A difficult, exhausting, strange gift, but a gift nonetheless.

"How are you feeling?" she asked as she watched Felicity take a seat at her mirror and pull out her earrings. Her dark lipstick had faded, eyeshadow smudged into dark patches.

Felicity shrugged. "Strange. Different. It's so terrible, and I suppose I should feel awful, but... I'm glad Timothy passed peacefully in the end."

"Me too," Blair nodded, inviting herself to perch on the edge of the bed. She could feel that Timothy was gone. Not completely — there would always be flickers of him here, just as there were of everyone who had existed — but that weight, that restlessness lingering about Hartwell, was gone. He'd finally found his peace tonight.

"It was you who allowed it to happen." Felicity turned around, brown eyes soft, warm, golden as the flames they reflected. Not as they had been once, so cold, so uninviting. When had she changed so much? When had she let Blair in, let her stay? "I'm sorry that I didn't believe you for so long, Blair. I'm sorry that I made such a mockery of you and accused you of such awful things. I was a fool for not seeing just how wonderful you were from the start."

The words left Blair's heart jittery and warm. Felicity thought she was wonderful. Felicity saw what Blair did, now. They had been linked tonight with something unbreakable, joined by the truth as well as their own hearts. Blair could trust Felicity. Felicity could trust Blair. Whatever had come before no longer mattered.

"Well, you warmed up to me in the end." Blair smiled crookedly, pushing off the bed to go back to Felicity. There was too much space between them, and to rectify the issue, Blair stepped between her legs, cupping her slender jaw in her hands. "That's what counts."

"You fixed something tonight I didn't even know was broken." The way Felicity blinked up at her from where she sat on her stool... it was almost enough for Blair to lose herself in. She had never been looked at that way before, as though she was magical or special or even remotely worth knowing. Not really. Not with the gravity Felicity did.

And it *was* gravity. It pulled Blair in, kept her grounded, and Blair hoped it would be just as permanent, though that wasn't guaranteed now. Her work here was done. She would have to go back to Birmingham, to pay the rent and visit her mother and see if anybody had requested her services while she was away. But the idea of that world, so dull and gray, so without Felicity... well, it could wait at least a night.

"I didn't fix anything," Blair murmured finally, wiping a stray tear from Felicity's cheek with the pad of her thumb. Her hands were still littered in cuts. "I just helped."

"It was so much more than that." Felicity's arms curled around Blair's waist, pulling her as close as possible, and yet there still felt to be too much between them. Too many clothes, too much space, too much skin. Blair had never wanted to make a home in another person, but if she could, it would be in Felicity, where the walls would be sturdy and the parlors would be full of silken pillows, hidden away with invitations only for the guests she trusted, and though the attic might have had shadows, it would not make her any less loveable.

Blair didn't know what they would be like together when they weren't solving mysteries or handling ghosts, but she would have quite liked to find out. Possibilities yawned out ahead of her, an endless corridor with so many doors to try.

"Come to bed," she whispered, not because of the niggling of lust beginning to tie itself around her gut but because she just *needed*. She needed Felicity in all of her forms, and she needed to enjoy the calm after the storm, and she needed to feel and see all of Felicity's sharp and soft edges without the shadows encroaching around them.

It wouldn't last long. Blair would always have another presence to feel, another person to help, another business to finish, and another grief to try to ease, but they had tonight. For tonight, it was just them.

So they lay together in the guttering light, darkness and fear and ghosts a thing of the past, as they should be. And for the first time since Blair had arrived, Hartwell Hall was peaceful.

Epilogue

A Temporary Parting of Ways

As it turned out, a message was left at the front desk for Blair just two days after they saw Timothy for the last time. Vincent had recommended her to one of his esteemed acquaintances, who was having trouble with strange occurrences in his pub in Leeds, and she had packed up her things by the end of the morning with a car waiting to take her to the train station.

They hadn't told Vincent everything about that night yet. It was Harold's story to tell, and his appearances around Hartwell had been scarce while he processed his decades-long grief. Still, he had come down to wish Blair farewell before she left, thanking her with a handshake and a brief glimpse of a smile. It had been more than Blair had been expecting.

Vincent wished her goodbye next and had even bought her a box of truffles for her troubles, which would probably be gone by the time she got to Leeds. Felicity had watched it all unfold quietly until it was her turn, and they waited until Vincent was called upon by a complaining Mrs. Walters — her Earl Grey tea had been mixed up with regular English breakfast, and they really *must* hire more competent staff — to say their goodbyes.

Blair didn't want to. Her throat bobbed with the promise of tears as she followed Felicity to the door, stopping just before the threshold. Felicity had taken her trunk of belongings. She placed it down now, rocking uncomfortably on her heels and looking anywhere but at Blair.

"So," she began. "Leeds. At least you'll be able to smoke freely in the pub."

"And the ashtrays will be clearly marked out, I'd wager," Blair teased, remembering that awful first meeting not so long ago. Somehow, she had made a fool of herself and yet had still wound up with Felicity's love and respect. "Thank you for everything you've done for me, Felicity. I won't forget it."

"I should be the one thanking you." Felicity's features were stretched thin. Blair had once thought it was hostility that lined her face like that, but now she knew better. Self-preservation. Pain. That's what it was. She knew because it matched the growing ache in Blair's chest. She wondered if her heart was trying to shrink; perhaps she would have less use of it now she was leaving without Felicity. As long as it had the chance to grow again when — *if* — they next saw one another, Blair didn't mind.

Blair smiled, but she could feel it didn't quite sit right on her own face. "We'll call it even, then."

"You know, Mr. Shaw complained about a funny smell in his room again last night. I think perhaps we have another ghost."

"Or perhaps he's been eating cabbage with his dinner."

"Maybe." A small chuckle that didn't sound right on Felicity's tongue.

Blair could barely breathe, and she wished Felicity would just *look* at her. Finally, she did, her eyes a maelstrom of emotions Blair didn't have time to identify. In the heart of it, though: sorrow. It was too soon. They'd only just found one another.

"Perhaps if we do experience some disturbances again, though, you might be willing to come back and offer your services? It's an old building. I'm sure there are plenty more ghosts."

Blair tutted, tucking a loose strand of dark hair behind Felicity's ear. She didn't particularly care who saw. They'd been walking around hand in hand for the last two days, and nobody had uttered a word, though Mrs. Walters had probably gossiped about them plenty in the taproom.

"You're so silly, Felicity," she said. "There doesn't need to be ghosts here for me to come back. If you want me, just ask."

Felicity chewed on her bottom lip, cheeks

flushing with color and perhaps want. But she was so proud, so stoic, and she merely clasped her hands together and pursed her lips.

"Just ask," Blair repeated: a plea now.

A jagged sigh fell from Felicity. "If I ask, I might never let you leave again."

Blair was quite alright with that idea, and to show it, she laced her fingers through Felicity's and pulled her closer. They shouldn't have fit together the way they did, physically or otherwise. Blair was tall and a little bit too busty, all soft-edged and fire. Felicity was ice, slim and sharp and covered in steel armor. And yet they melded into one another all the same, metal forged with flames, and Blair wouldn't have it any other way. She looked down at their entwined fingers, at where their stomachs met and their thumbs danced around each other's. She would miss this. Miss being this close to another soul. A soul who understood her, who knew all of her shadows and cobwebs and chose to let her stay anyway. But Blair had already been given much more than she could have ever expected here, and if she wanted to come back for it soon, she would need the money to do it. Living in Cheshire on a grand estate, after all, would cost slightly more than the shabby room she rented in Birmingham.

"I'll be back." To seal the promise, Blair brushed her nose against Felicity's.

"You'd better be," Felicity replied, with all of her usual authority. There was a crack in it somewhere, though, as though she wasn't sure if she could believe that they'd see one another again.

So Blair kissed her just in case her fears came to fruition, spilling over with all of the things there wasn't time to say yet. But there would be. She had worried before, but not now, not when it felt the rightest thing in Blair's universe to lose herself in Felicity.

A motorcar horn honked outside — her driver getting impatient. Blair tore herself away with regret, kissing Felicity on her forehead a final time before gathering her luggage.

"Just ask," she reminded.

"Just come back," Felicity said.

Blair smiled, because she would. And as she walked out of the doors of Hartwell Hall, she thought it strange that, of all the things she had uncovered here in her short stay, it was Felicity who had surprised her most — not the ghosts or the secrets or even Mrs. Walters's love for serenading everybody in the taproom each night.

Hauntings, she was used to, but the burning flame in her chest… that was new. And Blair would keep it ignited as long as Felicity would let her.

About the Author

Rachel Bowdler is a freelance writer, editor, and sometimes photographer from the UK. She spends most of her time away with the faeries. When she is not putting off writing by scrolling through Twitter and binge-watching sitcoms, you can find her walking her dog, painting, and passionately crying about her favourite fictional characters. You can find her on Twitter and Instagram @rach_bowdler.

Books By This Author

Handmade With Love

Partners In Crime

Paint Me Yours

Holding On To Bluebell Lodge

No Love Lost

Saving The Star

The Secret Weapon

Along For The Ride

The Fate Of Us

The Flower Shop On Prinsengracht

The Divide

Dance With Me

Printed in Great Britain
by Amazon